PRAISE FOR CATHERINE RYAN HYDE'S
FUNERALS FOR HORSES

"In this restrained but compelling narrative, Hyde movingly conveys the toll of years of emotional damage. Brutally lyrical."

—*Publishers Weekly*

"A rich blend of metaphors and genuine characters that will touch the hearts of readers. Highly recommended."

—*Library Journal* (Starred review)

"A true work of art . . . Enchanting."

—*The San Francisco Chronicle*

"Haunting."

—*The Washington Post Book World*

"Brilliantly wrought, finely plotted . . . Every scene is sketched with beautiful brevity . . . Every vista takes your breath away."

—*Small Press* (Featured review)

"Well worth reading."

—*New Times*

"Blunt, poetic [and] well-drawn."

—*San Luis Obispo Telegram-Tribune*

EARTHQUAKE WEATHER

CATHERINE RYAN HYDE

RussianHillPress • *San Francisco*

Russian Hill Press, San Francisco
www.russianhill.com
© 1998 by Catherine Ryan Hyde
All rights reserved. Published March 1998
Printed in the United States of America
00 99 98 97 5 4 3 2 1

The following stories have previously appeared as noted:

"Shoot for the Apex and Lean," from *The Crescent Review,* Fall/Winter 1994

"Alice Needs This," from *The Belletrist Review,* Spring/Summer 1994

"The Snake Handler," from *Bottomfish Magazine,* 1994 Annual

"Diogenes Jones," from *Pinehurst Journal,* Fall 1994

"Earthquake Weather," from *The South Dakota Review,* Fall 1994

"Mrs. Mulvany, the Grasshopper God," from *Pinehurst Journal,* Spring 1995

"Nicky Be Thy Name," from *The Belletrist Review,* Spring/Summer 1995

"Red Texas Sky," from *Eureka Literary Magazine,* Spring 1996

"Learning to Talk," from *Hayden's Ferry Review,* Fall 1995

"The Keeper," from *The Vignette,* Summer 1995

"Wednesday Man," from *Potpourri,* 1996

"Sam Will Remind Me," from *Flipside,* Fall 1996

"Paper Boy," from *Hayden's Ferry Review,* Fall/Winter 1996

"Blessing," from *Aura,* Winter 1997

"Lost Causes," from *Laurel Review,* January 1998

"Dante," from *Descant,* Spring 1997

"Love Is Always Running Away," from *The Amherst Review,* 1997

Book and jacket design by razor riders grp

This book is set in Minion and Futura

Library of Congress Cataloging-in-Publication Data
Hyde, Catherine Ryan
  Earthquake Weather / by Catherine Ryan Hyde
          -1st ed.
[97-076146]
CIP
ISBN 0-9653524-7-1

TABLE OF CONTENT

DANTE

*K*ennel man says, "Ever had a dog before?"

"When I was a kid we had a cocker spaniel."

"This ain't no cocker spaniel."

The dog is in a run by himself. He doesn't have to share with other dogs. Because he won't. "What kind of dog is he?"

"I dunno. No kind of dog. Every kind of dog. Got some hound, maybe. Maybe not."

He's yellow. Short hair, not shiny or lustrous. Strong looking. Ellen keeps thinking that. Not pretty; in fact, he gives her the creeps. He hasn't looked at her yet.

Kennel man says, "You gotta take him?"

"No. I don't have to."

"You gotta take him otherwise you don't get some big inheritance?"

"No. He is the inheritance. Just him."

"Lucky you. Don't take him."

"Why not?" She gets down on her knees in front of his chain-link gate. The dog makes a greater effort to avoid her eyes.

"I just don't trust that dog."

"Did he bite you?"

"No."

"Did he try?"

"No. But I can see him thinking about it. He's too smart."

"Too smart for who?"

"Look at his gate. Why do you think it's padlocked? He learned how to put his paw through and work the latch. So we put a clothespin on it. So he learns how to bite the clothespin so it opens. God did not intend dogs to be that smart."

God did not intend dogs, period, she thinks. They were our creation. But she doesn't care to argue theology. "Why is he so skinny? Don't you feed him?"

"Yeah, we feed him, but he don't eat."

"What's his name again?"

"Danty, I think. Something like that. It's on his card."

"Why don't you go get his card?"

As soon as she's alone with the dog, he turns his head and looks into her eyes. It's a chilling moment. His eyes are yellow. She feels reduced by his stare. He averts his gaze again, because the kennel man is back.

Ellen reads the card.

"Dante," she says. The dog's head whips around. His lip curls back to expose monumental fangs. He wags his whole body, grovels across cold concrete on his belly to the gate. "Why is he snarling at me?"

"I dunno, but he's wagging his tail. Maybe he's smiling. Some dogs do that when they feel cowed. You can tell he knows you. I'm glad he likes *somebody*."

She has never met this dog before.

Against her better judgment, she puts the back of her hand to the chain link, and he covers it with his wide tongue, gratefully.

"Open the gate," she says.

He drops the key onto the aisle floor beside her. "You open it." He clears the area before she can.

Dante leans out. Kisses her face excessively. It's not pure friendliness, there's something straining and desperate and apologetic about it.

She reaches in for his dish of untouched kibble, sits in the aisle on the cold concrete, Dante lying heavy on her legs, and he eats kibbles one at a time out of her hand.

There's something to be said for alcoholism, though I admit I've reached this conclusion vicariously. Carrie used to be an alcoholic, and she told me all about it. She says she still is, but that's beyond me. Alcoholics drink. Carrie doesn't.

After thirty white-knuckle days of not calling Grant, nobody gave me a nice little medallion to wear on my keychain. At the vast watershed of a year, no cake. Nobody sang. At Grant's memorial, even though I didn't know those people, I was sharply aware of their potential failure to appreciate that accomplishment. It wasn't as easy as it sounds.

We were on a hill, this bunch of strangers and me, looking out over Mariner's Cove. A string quartet played, because Grant loved classical music. Of course he did. I never knew that about him until that moment. I remember being glad I'd never played Elvis Costello when he was over. Somehow I thought I'd left Grant just in time to avoid that moment where I realize I don't know him. That's kind of a joke though, because I remember why I finally broke it off. You're with a man for almost two years, you should know where he lives, and you should have met his dog. Even I can see that's not natural.

You get angry, thinking about what you don't know.

There was one familiar face there, but I tried to avoid it. His name was Wilson Greene. He introduced me to Grant; he hadn't quite gotten over the fact that something came of that introduction; and I hadn't quite forgiven him for starting the rolling snowball of events. When I saw him coming, I tried to duck.

Meanwhile I was thinking *this is all wrong. Crashing surf and strains of classical music. In my family, we had organ music and a lot of screaming and crying. This is way too genteel.* My thoughts become disjointed in stress situations.

Wilson put his hand on my arm. "We have to talk, Ellen."

"Funny, we never did before."

"About the will. I'm the executor, you know."

"You? Not his wife?" Please don't tell me which one she is.

"Maybe because of this odd situation . . ."

"Are you saying Grant left me money? I am not going to sit in on a reading of the will and watch the look on his wife's face. I'm sorry. Tell them I died." A slight exaggeration. Please don't tell me which one she is.

"It's not money."

Real property, a car, a personal effect of some sort. A problem either way. Then it hit me. I knew it was true, because it matched the look on Wilson's face. "Oh, god. The dog."

"You knew about it."

"What does his wife think about that?"

"She hates the dog."

That doesn't entirely answer the question. Please don't tell me which one she is. "What's the dog's name?"

"You never met his dog?"

"Where exactly is this dog right now?"

"In a private kennel. See, technically he's in probate. I think they said his name was Dandy. Something like that."

Dandy? Grant's dog? I think not. "So, listen, Wilson." I put an arm around his shoulder, turned him back to face the stately congregation. "Tell me. Which one is his wife?"

They cross the fence line together. She unclips the leash. Since leaving Grant, she's moved to a rural locale. Life here is not as simple as she had hoped. For the first time, they see cattle, glimpses of them lumbering between scrawny pine and scrub oak. Foraging. Dante gathers like a crossbow. Launches. In the second of gathering, she notices his build. His barrel. Rangy but muscular. Such a powerful machine. It frightens her, even though he's on her side. A loaded gun in her hand would be on her side, but its potential would frighten her.

She screams his name.

This is private grazing land. They shouldn't, technically, be here. But she can't take the dog around other animals, and he needs to run. And Dwight said she could. Dwight, he stays in the caretaker's cabin. He's a close friend, Dwight. Very close. He said she could, if the dog doesn't run cattle.

"If he runs cattle, keep him home or I'll have to shoot him."

"If he runs cattle I'll keep him home."

As she crashes through the brush, screaming his name, he comes crawling back. Her voice is like an earthquake to him. Slithering through pine needles and poison oak on his belly, showing his teeth. She's still not comfortable with that, though it's clearly passive. Grovels at her feet, licking her shoes. She never yelled at him before, and now she wonders if he'll ever get over it.

They walk on to Dwight's cabin, Dante bounding ahead. A short parade of cattle wanders across the road. Dante freezes, stares at the dirt close-range until they survey him and move on.

They arrive at Dwight's cabin. Dwight meets them out front.

Dante puts his head down, growls low in his throat. She has yet to find someone Dante likes, but he likes Dwight less than most. Already.

"Well," she says. "He doesn't run cattle, that's for sure."

"Good watchdog."

"I'll say." She has begun to fear that in Dante's presence, nothing bad, or good, will ever happen to her.

Dwight approaches carefully, one hand extended. Goes down on one knee. Speaking low, offers the back of his hand. Dante's lip peels back differently. He snarls, leaps forward to attack the air, biting down less than an inch from Dwight's hand. More show of teeth, and a long, rolling growl. Dwight pulls back in slow motion, white-faced.

Dante sits at Ellen's heel, leaning.

Dwight throws her a chain—a big, heavy one, the sort you'd use to haul a car out of the mud. She chains Dante to a tree and joins Dwight on the porch. As she walks into his arms, the yelping splits the air like a scream. They watch the dog hit the end of his chain and flip over onto his back, repeatedly, mouth foaming with the sweat of his exertion.

Dwight says, "I do believe that dog is crazy."

"I better go get him."

"Hell, no. You want him to run you?"

"I guess not."

She follows him inside, where he undresses her, and pins her to his bed, like so many times before. His pants are halfway off, hobbling him around the knees, when something slams against his door. From the sound, something about the size of a tractor.

"Shit," Dwight says. He stands up and trips over his pants.

They can hear Dante chewing at the door. Tearing at the door. Dwight kicks a leg out of his pants and runs to the window, his urgency mirroring her own. If Dante wants in, she figures he'll get in. Dwight pulls back the curtain, and the shadow, the shape, crashes against the glass, shatters it, but bounces off again. Dwight locks himself in the bathroom before the next, successful leap.

Dante hits the bathroom door once, as if for effect, then stands with his head down, growling, intimidating it.

"Dante!" He jumps onto the bed beside her, slapping his tail. Kisses her face. She checks him for damage. Blood, some, on his face and one leg. Nothing deep or dangerous looking. "Oh, Dante. You broke your collar."

Dante rests his head between his front paws in shame.

"Ellen? What are you doing?"

"Getting dressed." Having said so, she gets started on that.

"Ellen? I really think the best thing for everybody would be if you let me shoot that dog."

"Everybody but him, you mean."

"You figure on keeping him?"

Dante's eerie yellow eyes come up to meet hers. He must have heard everything. "He's a good watchdog."

"Yeah, well, either he goes or I do."

She pulls on her sweater, and Dante curls around her legs all the way out the door. "It's been real," she says.

Dwight sends her a bill for the damage; she pays it without comment.

I dwell on the past. Always have.

Lying in bed with Grant. After. My mind a perfect blank, because that's how it always was. My body and head hollow, humming, like a tuning fork almost ready to go still. But not quite. My eyes closed.

It was always better than great with Grant, but mostly with my eyes closed, because none of his greatness was visible. So I wondered, sometimes, if I was imagining, manufacturing the good parts. I never held tangible proof of their existence.

When I first told Carrie she said, "Ooh. Tell me all about him. Is he young? Is he handsome? Is he hung?"

Even one out of three might have redeemed me, but as it was, I didn't answer.

"So, the sex is, like, great, right?"

"Phenomenal."

"That's something."

Anyway, we were lying there, his mouth against my ear, a good moment for tender words, if that had ever been Grant's style. "If anything happens to me, Ellen, I want you to take my dog."

Don't talk, Grant. Just enjoy the moment. It's gone so long, in between. "Nothing will happen to you. Don't be silly."

"If it does."

"Everybody outlives their dog. That's why I don't get one."

"Doctor thinks I'm ripe for an M.I. Cholesterol, blood pressure. Family history. For starters. I'm not a kid, Ellen."

"Can we talk about something else? After you tell me what an M.I. is?"

"Myocardial infarction."

"Like a heart attack."

"Exactly like one."

"Then why don't you just say heart attack?"

By this time he was putting on his clothes. He'd stayed longer than usual. "Just promise me."

"Wouldn't your wife want the dog?"

"No. She wouldn't. Promise me."

I wanted to, because I always wanted to be what he wanted. Helpful. Intelligent. Loyal. I felt like a Girl Scout in his presence. Grant died owing me a handful of merit badges I worked hard for and will never see.

"I've never even met your dog, Grant."

"Well, you'll have to, then."

"Bring him with you when you come next week."

"Okay, I will."

But he didn't.

We went to bed; it was phenomenal, as always, even though I knew what I would say when it was over. I knew if he didn't bring the dog, that was the last straw.

I didn't call to change my mind. I guess I thought if I could hold out long enough, it would be that great with somebody else.

The need for him cycled like a recurring fever, hid around corners waiting to trip me. Swept me offshore like a rip current. The missing him. It sang to me, an opiate drug reminding me how warm and familiar it had always felt, could always feel again. How easy it would be to fall back into. But I didn't call. Thinking the universe would reward my resolve.

It's never been that good with anybody else. And god knows I've tried. At least it was over before I promised to take the damned dog I'd never met. It irked me that I'd forgotten to ask the dog's name. There's always one thing you can't let go of, and it's usually something peripheral and fairly unimportant. I guess it's easier that way.

Carrie says, "Maybe you should change his name. It might make him sound friendlier."

Ellen says, "I don't think the issue is how he sounds." She sits on the floor by the window with her arm around the dog. They both hold still because Carrie is sketching them for a portrait. Dante seems to understand the art of posing. Dante seems to understand everything. Ellen is beginning to think the kennel man was right. Maybe there's only just so smart a dog should be. "What do you think I should call him?"

Carrie seems to consider this, and when she decides, Ellen knows by her smile. "Grant's Revenge."

"Right. Friendly. I don't want to change his name."

"Do you think that's why he had you take him?"

"What do you mean?" She knows what Carrie means. She's considered it herself, at some length.

"How long since you've been with a man?"

"Five or six months."

"For real, Ellen." It's a little game they play.

"Okay, seven months, thirteen days. Not counting that one time. With that one guy. Who didn't deserve to be counted."

At first it seemed rational to think she'd leave the dog at home and go to his place, whoever he was. But she has not succeeded in leaving the dog alone. He'll get out, and follow.

Through a window if necessary. So she takes him places with her, or she gets Carrie to babysit.

Since leaving the city, she works at home, on the internet. Thank god.

Potentially she could leave the dog with Carrie and go to his place, but Carrie has a life, too, and Ellen hasn't found a *him* who doesn't consider that a burdensome limitation.

"So, do you think that's why Grant did it?"

"No. I think it was because nobody else would have kept the dog." She realizes that if she were to die, she'd have to obligate someone to Dante, too.

"So in other words, Grant's dead, and you're still being the one person he can always count on."

"Don't artists usually like silence when they work?"

"You should think about getting rid of him."

Dante breaks the pose. Slinks, and pushes his head onto Ellen's lap.

"Who, Grant or the dog? I wish you would be careful what you say around him."

"He doesn't speak English."

"He knows what people are thinking. Look at him."

"Now I have to be careful what I think around him?"

"I can't get rid of him. He doesn't like anybody else. Except you."

"Well, don't look at *me*." She folds up her sketchpad, ending the session. Maybe she'll work from a photograph. That was the original plan. Before Dante proved himself a poser. "So, he'd have to be put to sleep or something. I know. That's hard. But . . ."

"Can we talk about something else? You're really freaking him out." Dante has crawled over her lap and is trying to hide between Ellen and the window, but she's not big enough to provide the cover he needs. "Maybe I'll have to try women."

"He doesn't like women either."

"No, that's true. Just you."

"Definitely don't look at me." She swings her coat on, stands by the door.

"Don't worry. He doesn't like you as much as he used to."

"Is this about the dog, Ellen? Or is this about Grant?"

She has to think. She doesn't like questions that make her think. She likes Carrie for hardly ever asking them. "Because he loves me. And because I loved Grant."

Carrie's eyebrows react. "I thought that was mostly sex."

"Yeah. Me too." Until she tried to replace it.

"I'll call you," Carrie says as the door swings shut.

When her footsteps are gone, Dante sits up. She puts her arms around him. Feels a slight tremble in his muscles as she holds him.

"We both miss him. Huh, Dante?"

She gets up quickly to make a cup of tea, unable to identify what that will solve. How tea will be an antidote for loss.

Dante whines, long and low, and when she's left the room, he looses a long, modulated, unnerving howl which raises goosebumps on her skin—and leaves her thinking that she can never find just the right words.

Lately I've been troubled by vivid limited memories of Grant, and they make me worry about love. I don't like so many questions being raised at a time in my life when I feel I should have some answers.

One thing I know for sure about love. It's a bitch of a thing to identify in retrospect. Concerning a dead man. But I guess dead or married—it's all the same to me at the bottom line. Only, dead is safer.

In one memory, I come up on him sitting in a chair, putting his socks on, and I kiss the top of his forehead, where I'm sure he had hair in his youth, but not much at the time. Something else to fault him for, but it doesn't work. I remember his chest, easing down on me. This must be a sexier thought if the guy had a flatter, tighter stomach. Less hair on his chest and more on his head. But Dwight was young, handsome and hung and I don't think about him much anymore.

It's not that I like older, balder, smaller, soft-muscled men better, because the world is full of them if that was the only problem. It's something about the exact sum of Grant, like a DNA strand, and any substitution seems to ruin the equation.

See, I worry that I might have just described love.

I met a guy who didn't seem to feel my strange dog was an undue hardship. In fact, I think he respected that about me. So I told him at great length how I happened to come by Dante. When I was sure he would never call me again, my relief felt so tangible that I had to admit I did it on purpose.

Carrie says, "I changed my mind. I don't think you should get rid of the dog. I think this might be good for you."

Ellen says, "What do you mean?" She knows what Carrie means. She has considered it herself, at some length.

"How old is that dog?"

"He's supposed to be about seven. Maybe eight by now."

"So, he'll live to be about ten, right?"

"Or twelve. Or fourteen."

"Anyway, the town just voted you least likely to get robbed or raped. That's something."

"Yeah, that's something. I'm certified uneventful."

Ellen moves to a different house in an even more remote location.

She hopes Dante lives to be fifteen, at least. More time to think.

THE SNAKE HANDLER

I try to dust the living room, but his eyes follow me like a painting from a haunted house.

I wax the dining room table and think how the name Forrest doesn't suit him. A forest is green and natural, infused with life and balance.

It's before seven AM. I never do housework this early. What's come over me? I can't hold still in his presence. I want my life back the way it was before. I stick my head out into the living room again, only to meet his deadly gaze head on.

"I wish you'd stop staring at me like that."

He shrugs and turns on the television, and I hear the familiar lisp of Daffy Duck's cartoon dialogue. I snapped at him. I never snap at anyone. He's been living with us for a matter of hours, and my personality has changed. His eyes are focused away now, and I take the opportunity to stare.

He wears only jeans, props his bare feet up on the couch. His dark hair frames his face in an uncivilized way, somewhere between seldom combed and dreadlocks. He has that *thing* wrapped around his arm, that vile digestive tract with scales he calls a pet. On his other arm is a tattoo of a coiled snake. The scary thing is, I see Christopher in him—a dark part of Chris, like something split away in a bizarre genetic accident.

I lock myself in the bedroom and call Chris at work.

"Old Town Bakery."

"I thought you said he'd keep that thing in a cage."

"So what's it doing? Slithering around the house?"

"He's watching TV and it's wrapped around his arm."

"So tell him to put it back in the cage."

Tell him, I think. Just like that. Easy. Like walking up to a gangbanger in a dark alley and shouting orders. "I thought I wasn't going to have to deal with discipline things."

"But I'm at work, Darcy. What can I do from here? You got a problem with the kid, you've got to work it out."

"He's not a kid," I say. "He's nineteen. Old enough to vote. Hold a job. Live alone." As I hear myself say it, I realize I sound no less carping than I did on our last trip through this same issue. I hate myself this way, but I'm out of alternatives. Already.

"Please, Darcy. I'm behind schedule. I just got a special order for ten dozen croissants. I'll be here 'til noon as it is. Do your best with him 'til I get back, okay?" When I don't answer he says, "Love you."

When I know he's hung up, I slam down the phone.

I ease down the stairs, peer into the living room, but the TV is off, the room quiet. No Forrest. I check the kitchen, but it's empty. When I turn, he's behind me: suddenly, heart-stoppingly *there*, the evil reptile draped on his shoulders.

"Boo," he says in a quiet deadpan.

I lock myself in the bedroom until Chris comes home.

It's three AM and I can't sleep. I used to be a good sleeper, no, better than good. I pull on jeans and a sweater and drive to the shop. I need the company.

Chris opens the back door. He has donut dough on the table, a bad time for distractions. He doesn't look happy to see me.

"Thought we weren't going to do this, Darcy."

He makes it so damned hard to say I need you. "I couldn't sleep."

"But this is my time. We agreed on that, right?"

He doesn't use a lot of light for his baking, just the lights above the oven and the glow of the refrigerated cases. His face is a familiar comfort. His dark eyes are deeply set behind a heavy forehead. Like his son. His hair is gray at the sides but short on top, as though a young haircut, a young wife, will save him from time.

I argue my fear of staying home all night with his son, but he isn't having it. Maybe he thinks I'm only quarreling to avoid going home. Maybe he's right. I leave without saying goodbye.

Home, I walk through a darkened living room.

Forrest's voice is a gunshot in the dark. "He doesn't like that, does he?"

I gasp and put a hand to my chest, a gesture he fortunately cannot see. Then the struggle to breathe again, to somehow sound unrattled.

"Who? Like what?"

"My dad. He doesn't like it when you drop by the shop."

"How do you know where I've been?" Windmills of irrational thought. He followed me. He has psychic powers. Black magic.

"Not a whole lot open in this town at night." I breathe again, try to feel my way to the bedroom. I should have left lights on, but I didn't want to wake him. Alert him, rather. "So, you wanta know *why* he doesn't?"

I grope for the kitchen light switch. In the spill of half-light, Forrest sits on the living room couch, wearing only boxer shorts. I wish he wouldn't do that, but I'd be embarrassed to say so. He works out, and it shows. His eyes fix me not with pure anger, but with an angry version of hunger. Intensity. Sexuality, I think; but maybe I read that in.

"What could you possibly know about my marriage?"

"Look, you've known him—what? A year? I've known him all my life. He's into privacy, only maybe you don't know details. If you want, I'll tell you why my mother divorced him. If you don't, I won't."

"Your mother did not divorce Chris—he divorced her."

"Hell, I was there, lady."

"Don't call me lady!"

I storm through the dining room, bump a heavy glass pitcher and send it flying, then somehow save it before it hits the hardwood floor. I hold it in my hands for a split second, then smash it against the far dining room wall.

I want my life back the way it was before.

Forrest appears in the doorway as I gather the pieces. I don't want him to see. I don't do things like this. I slice my thumb, and blood wells up and drops to the floor. He brings me a paper towel. I thank him, and wrap my thumb with it, my face held down, so he won't see the angry tears.

When Chris comes home I'm still in bed, though it's after ten. "How's my lady?" he says. The word sounds different coming from him. He takes off his whites, climbs in beside me. He smells of hot grease. I lie on my back, arms behind my head.

"Tell me again about your split with Marilyn. Your idea?"

His big, square hand slides across my belly. "Kind of a mutual thing, I guess."

It starts as a knot in my insides, a twisting. "That's not how you explained it. You said you left *her.*"

"Well, you know. There's a lot of sides to these things. Divorce is complicated." He says this with irritating authority, because I've never been married before. He likes subjects where I have to take his word.

He wants to make love but I'm not in the mood.

By the seventh day Forrest's eyes have changed, the animosity replaced by a strange approval, as though he's seeing me on purpose. I liked him better before. He still refuses to wear a shirt in the house. He never goes out.

I used to sunbathe in the yard, but I've taken to using the terrace outside the bedroom window for privacy. Today I open my eyes to see him standing over me, complete with snake. I scramble to my feet and pull a towel around me— overkill, I realize. I dress this way on the beach in front of strangers. But Forrest is not a stranger. That's the problem.

"Don't *ever* come through that bedroom door without knocking."

"I knocked. You didn't hear me."

"I come out here for privacy."

"I'm sorry. I'm going to walk to the store; I just came to ask if you wanted anything."

It's out of character, and I don't believe him. He never walks to the store. What does he use for money? Is Chris giving him money? To call his bluff, I say, "Maybe a six-pack of soda."

"Okay, fine." For a split second I think his eyes look hurt, but I must be dreaming.

When he gets home he knocks louder. I'm still on the terrace, but in my beach robe. He sits on a canvas chair, peels off his shirt, pops the top on a can of soda and hands one to me.

"You're too good for this," he says.

"For what?"

"Him."

"Look, don't start on your father. I won't listen."

"That's just the problem. I'm trying to help. And you won't listen."

"I don't want to hear you put him down."

"I'm not putting him down. It's just a fact. I don't even think it's something he can help. He just has a problem with women. Kind of a sickness."

"What do you mean, a problem with women?" I hear and feel myself bristle. I don't want to hear these lies, but I want him to clarify which lies I don't want to hear.

"He just can't stop having them."

"I think you should go now."

"Hardly a day went by he didn't cheat on my mother."

"You're a sick young man, Forrest." He only smiles. "You're an evil liar." It sounds weak, the way I say it.

"True. All true. Only this time I'm not lying."

But when a liar says he isn't lying, do you believe him? I tell him to get out, and he does.

Chris comes home at noon. I sandbag him.

"I want him out."

"Darcy, we've been through this."

"I want him *out*, Chris! Send him back to his mother."

"She can't handle him."

"Neither can I!"

I hear the sound of Forrest's stereo, suddenly cranked to an unreasonable volume, and I realize he's trying to drown us out.

"I can't put him out on the street. He's got problems."

"The biggest favor you could do for him is to force him to make his own way. Sooner or later he'll have to."

"Look, Darcy, he's practically unemployable. And he doesn't take his lithium when he's on his own. What happened, anyway?"

I breathe deeply, fight with the tears. They win.

"He's telling lies about you."

"Well, that's not such a big deal, is it? Just don't listen. He's the one with the emotional problems. We have to keep a little more perspective."

He wraps his arms around me, and the tears let loose all at once, all out of control. I say, "I just want my life back the way it was before."

He kisses me, and walks me backwards to the bed, and eases me down. In the silence, the stereo drops to normal volume, and as we make love on our squeaky bed, against the wall to Forrest's room, the music blasts again.

Four AM. I wake from the strangest, most terrifying dream— about a half-man, half-snake. Big as a man, with a tail curling down to nothing in mid-air, no part of him touching the ground, as if energy will hold him up. I run into the house to escape him, then hear him throw his huge body against the door. Then I open up and let him in. Who knows why? It's a dream, right? I see the cold, metallic gleam of his inhuman eyes, and I wake sitting upright in bed.

As I sit, wheezing for breath, the bedroom door flies open and I scream. Framed in the doorway, I see the silhouette of Forrest, in boxer shorts.

"You okay, Darcy?"

"I'm . . . what? Of course I'm okay. Why?"

"You were yelling about something."

"Oh. Was I? A dream, is all."

He moves toward my bed, one hand out, as if to . . . help? Attack? I'm beyond knowing. I flatten my back against the headboard, listening to the panic in my voice as if through someone else's ears. "No! Just go, okay?"

When he's gone I lock the door.

In the morning Forrest walks to the beach. I watch him through the window, from the second floor, feeling the weight in my belly shift and change with his distance.

I open the door to his room; I'm not sure why. The snake is confined to a big wire cage, about the size of a kennel run for a medium-size dog. It notices my presence immediately. Its tongue flicks out, feeling the air for me, and it begins to "pace." It slithers from one side of the enclosure to the other, raising its head and neck almost two feet off the ground, suspended in the air, staring with cold, unblinking eyes. I slam the door again.

This evening I stop at a local coffee house because, I tell myself, I don't get out enough. Tonight a dream therapist holds court on the back patio. I knew that. At some point I knew that, but I tell myself it isn't why I came.

She's a soft, heavy old woman with drooping eyes and a gentle manner. She sits against the faded stone wall under a labyrinth of bare vines. She talks about compensatory dreams and prophetic dreams, but little of dream symbolism. She seems to feel each dream has a fairly direct meaning, based in some degree on the events of the previous day.

A young Asian man asks questions. He lost his girlfriend because he caught her cheating. "But I'm young," he says, "so I don't care." Now, however, he dreams about her. In the dreams, he cares.

His words roll over and over in my brain. What does being young have to do with anything? Everybody cares about that. Everybody hurts. I watch his baby-faced profile, and, as he doesn't know he hurts, I hurt for him.

A thin middle-aged woman raises her hand. She says a dream analyst in Napa Valley told her never to tell her dreams to anyone, because you have no idea how much they reveal.

I walk out, leaving half my cafe mocha in the glass. I glance over my shoulder at the tables of college students and locals, and realize I haven't made any friends in this town.

When I get home, I call Karen.

"How's life in the sticks?" she says.

I tell her about Forrest. I do not share details of my dream.

But in a move which surprises even me, I share Forrest's lies about Chris. "Everything was so perfect before he came."

Karen laughs at me. "Perfect? This from the woman who cried on my shoulder because Chris wanted to dump a successful practice, leave the city and stay up all night baking bread? You said you married one man, but they wrapped the wrong one to go."

"Well, I know, but . . . I can understand him. A lot of men want their own business. He wanted to work with his hands, see a real product for his efforts."

"What does understanding have to do with it, though? You hate it. Same thing with Forrest. What do you care what Chris's reasons are for having him? It's ruining your life, right?"

After a certain amount of runaround, I admit it. The lies are ruining me.

"How do you know he's lying?"

I'm too stunned to speak. My first reflex is to hang up on her. I push through the initial stutters, say, "Of course it's a lie. How can you even say that?"

"You're not answering my question." She explains that I'm an ostrich of an individual, or she wouldn't subject me to the idea. "Let's say there's a ten percent chance he's telling the truth."

"No. Zero percent."

"Let's just say. So you subject your marriage to a little scrutiny. If it's a solid marriage, nothing to lose, right?"

I tell her I have to go, that Forrest is home. Forrest has been home all along, locked in his room. I make a mental note to get out more, make new friends. The old ones aren't working out.

At two thirty AM I drive into town and park around the corner from the shop. I set up in the alley, separated from the bakery parking lot by a five-foot board fence. Hidden in the moon shadows of an oak tree, I lean and watch. With every breath, I think, why? Why am I doing this? To satisfy Karen? Forrest? Or does some part of me actually doubt?

My heart swells and thumps and feels heavy. He crosses the window on every trip to the oven. Alone. What did I expect?

I drive home, feeling defeated because I stooped to checking up on him.

In the living room, Forrest sprawls on the couch in a pair of cut-off jeans. Only the light of the television screen reveals him. He watches a mad scientist perform a head transplant. I cast a look back over my shoulder, catch something in his eyes that scares me, but I can't place it. I try to fix myself a glass of juice, but as I close the refrigerator door I collapse, as though a sudden leak steals all my air. I slide down with my back against the door, breathing as though crying, but my eyes are dry. I can't believe I almost took his word against my own husband. I can't believe I've been reduced to this.

When I look up, Forrest is crouched over me, his eyes deep and soft, like I've never seen them, never guessed I would.

"I'm sorry, Darcy."

He tries to touch my hair, but I flinch away. So, he admits it. All lies. I knew that but never expected to hear it from him. I look up into his face, and I almost ask: Why, Forrest? Why would you try to drive a wedge between Chris and me? Before I can ask, I know. It's right there in his eyes. And it's not the first time I've seen it, just the first moment it sinks in.

I'm flattered, repelled, drawn to it, afraid of it, all at the same time. I put a hand on his bare chest, push him away from me. It catches him off guard, knocks him back onto the kitchen linoleum, where he remains, sprawled, looking helpless, like something beached.

I run out of the room, the house.

I run to Chris. So I can tell him how I almost believed it, so he can forgive me. How I'm sorry I doubted him, even for a split second, which is all the doubting I did.

But the bakery is dark. Chris' car is in the parking lot, but it seems that no one is there. Maybe he ran down to the warehouse, I think, and as I back my car out of the lot, a light comes on over the oven. I see my husband, buttoning his shirt. I hit the gas, still in reverse, and back all the way into the service station across the deserted street. I kill my lights.

A few minutes later the back door opens, and by the light of the streetlamp I see Jenny, the college girl who works early mornings behind the counter. Chris appears at the door behind her, looks both ways, then pulls her in for a long goodbye kiss.

When I get home, Forrest is asleep. I burst into his room,

throw the door open so hard it hits the wall. He jumps half into a sitting position, tries to scramble awake, out of bed. I flip on the light and he blinks. He looks smaller somehow. Maybe he *is* a kid.

"Darcy? What the hell—"

"You weren't lying. Were you?"

"No. I told you."

"Why did you apologize to me?"

"Apologize?" He shakes his head as if to remove excess sleep. "I didn't. I just said I was sorry. That you got hurt. I didn't want to be the one to tell you. Just hated to see you get done over, like my mom."

I take a long, deep breath and sit down on his floor. I don't know what I feel. Maybe I feel nothing. Maybe I feel too many emotions, all lined up like planes on a runway, and nothing can get through.

He wraps the sheet around his waist, comes and sits on the floor beside me. For the longest time he says nothing, does nothing. Then he puts one awkward arm around my shoulder. I crumble into tears. I cry until I don't ever want to cry again. Until it feels like a chore, and I'm too tired. Then I laugh, I don't know at what.

"Has that thing got a name?" I say. I gesture to the snake, which is watching us with careful rhythm.

"It's a he. His name is Basil. Basil Ratbones."

I laugh again, but this time I know why. I say, "You're too young to remember an old-time actor like that. But I should be, too."

"Hey, I'm quite a Sherlock Holmes fan. Read all the books, seen all the movies."

"Really? I didn't know that about you." I didn't know Forrest had read any book, ever.

"There's lots you don't know about me. You never asked. You never acted like you wanted to know." He's right, and I admit it. "It's not his fault, really. I mean, it is and it isn't. It's like a sickness with him. Don't take it personal."

I laugh bitterly. I say, "Murderers and rapists are sick, too, but you still tend to take it personally."

"I know," he says. "I hate him for what he did to my mother. Know what he did to me once? He promised to take me to a football game. And we went out for ice cream sundaes first, and at the soda shop, he met this girl, and they got to talking. We never made it to the game. I ended up sitting in a hotel lobby all afternoon, waiting for him."

"How old were you, Forrest?"

"Nine."

His face is too close to mine, I'm seeing it too close up, and I know he's just a boy who's been through too much. Maybe that's all Chris is, but I can't afford to think that way right now. I touch his face and am surprised to feel whiskers. He tries to kiss me, and just for a minute I let him. No, not a minute. A second. Maybe long enough to count to two. Then I'm on my feet.

"No, Forrest. Don't even think it."

"I have a right to *think* it," he says, his eyes cast down to the carpet.

"Don't try to make it happen."

"If I promise, will you stay?"

I sit with him again. Because I need his arm around me, someone's arm, and only Forrest is here.

I say I'm sorry I called him evil, and a liar. And a sick young man. He says it doesn't matter, it's all close enough to the truth.

We sit awake all night, talking, and he tells me other things about himself that I wouldn't have guessed.

Chris comes in at noon. I haven't slept.

"You got behind schedule," I say.

"Yeah, some." He jumps onto the bed beside me, bounces up and down on the creaky springs. He's too cheerful. It's not that he doesn't know I'm upset. He knows. He probably thinks something happened with Forrest. He doesn't want to hear about it. He's ready to jolly me out of it.

I'm ready to let him.

I don't know where it comes from, but it's here in full force. If I say nothing, today will be just like yesterday. The only difference is that I know. Maybe I can unknow. Maybe just for a minute, or a day.

He climbs under the covers with me, and some part of me hovers just below the ceiling, watching. It says, have you no self-respect? I don't answer. I let him kiss me, and I kiss back. I hope that's not the answer.

The emotion of the night flips over into need and energy, and I pull him down with me, because I'm not ready to let him go. I hear our creaky bedsprings but no music, nothing to drown us out. I can't bear to think of Forrest knowing. Or anyone. This is no time to see myself through anyone's eyes.

In time I hear a noise, a pounding, like the bed banging against the wall, but it's not that. It's too loud and muffled, too irregular. It comes from Forrest's side. I picture Forrest pounding his head against our wall.

"What's wrong?" Chris asks, and I realize I'm lying still, listening.

I wonder, doesn't he hear that? Doesn't he care? I tell him I lost the mood, and I get up and leave the room.

I nap on the couch until he goes off to work again, and the dream comes back, the snake-man, and again I open the door and let him in.

I wake after midnight, and pack a few things. As I load them into the car, I see Forrest standing in the open doorway behind me, watching. He comes out onto the stoop, sits on a stone stair. I worry that he must be cold.

I walk back to him.

"You haven't asked me where I'm going."

"Don't have to. You're going away where I won't see you."

I nod, because I can't make the right words happen. I want to thank him for ruining my life. No, that's wrong. But he'd probably know what I mean.

"What do you think he'll say when he gets home and I'm gone?"

He shrugs. "Doesn't matter anymore. Does it?"

"No, you're right," I say. "It doesn't."

To avoid his eyes, I stare at the knot of purple and green bruise on his forehead. I reach my fingers out, almost touch it, but not quite.

SHOOT FOR THE APEX AND LEAN

*P*atterson's windshield is cracked. He's peered through it too long, which explains some of his problems.

He drives eighty-eight down Turrey Road, into the curve where Amigo did his trick. Only not in an old step-side pickup, he didn't. But then, Amigo was stone drunk. Patterson is stone sober, which explains some of his problems.

Throw the wheel, stomp the brakes. The truck spins, like Amigo's Trans Am spun, only wider.

He slides into the westbound lane, facing back the way he came, two tires spinning and whining over the edge. He looks down the embankment to the barbed wire of a cattle fence, sure he is going down. He is not going anywhere. With two tires engaged he throws dirt, nothing more.

He rests his forehead on the wheel.

"So, Patterson," he says, "are we a man yet?"

Fortunately, he doesn't answer. He wishes Amigo was here. Amigo would get him unstuck.

Patterson hunches against a front tire of his old Chevy step-side and lights another of Amigo's smokes. He had quit, but has unquit. He smokes only half, because it makes him sick. He knocks the glowing tip off into the dirt.

Amigo says, "Shit." The word rises like sickening smoke from under the dented hood. Amigo still tries to push the spline of this newly acquired engine into the Chevy's bellhousing. Patterson has long since accepted that it does not fit, that it will never fit. Amigo has yet to accept.

Patterson flicks Amigo's lighter and torches the second half of the Marlboro. He knows it will make him sicker. He doesn't mind.

Amigo's wife is not home. Amigo's wife is never home. This is fine with Patterson. This seems fine with Amigo, probably because he does not smoke or drink beer in her presence. Amigo's wife left him last month but he found her in Atascadero and wooed her back.

"I'm going to stop lying to her," he told Patterson the following morning. Then, before Patterson left, Amigo asked him to take the bag of beer bottles home to recycle.

Amigo's wife was not home the night Patterson blew the Chevy's engine, out on the highway below Hearst Castle. He and Amigo were playing a game called "pushing the tach." Patterson heard the noise in the engine, but the oil pressure gauge was okay. He never asked Amigo why the gauge should read fine in a state of no oil, because he felt he should know.

A ranger loaned Patterson an orange cone, and in time Amigo cruised back down the coast to get him, and they ditched Patterson's fractured ride and spun up toward Ragged Point, where they parked, where Amigo drank seven beers to his two, where Amigo allowed him something.

Amigo asks nothing of Patterson, offers nothing, only allows. What he allows is not later discussed.

The sun left a dark stain of orange on the sharp line of ocean, and Amigo cranked up the radio to better hear Van Halen play "Come On Baby Finish What You Started." Amigo has a new bumper sticker. It says, WHEN LIFE THROWS YOU A CURVE, SHOOT FOR THE APEX AND LEAN.

Now Amigo pulls his head out from under the Chevy's hood and twists the top off another Bud. Bends it on itself like a little metal football. Flips it into the bed of the old abandoned Ford they hijacked for its leaf springs.

"I'll be damned, boy."

"Doesn't fit?"

"Can't get the damn spline to engage."

"Call up that guy in Morro Bay. That machine shop."

As Amigo steps into the house, Patterson notices shiny metallic balloons in the living room, swaying over a vase of flowers. One says *I love you*, another *Please forgive me*. The breeze shifts them to reveal the wedding photo on the wall behind. The sleeves are too long on Amigo's tux.

Just as the sun comes up. That's Patterson's favorite time in his woods. He gets paid to keep people out, by the man whose cattle graze here. He startles deer and moves fallen trees off the road, such as it is. He writes letters to Amigo in his head. Later he writes them down. Then cuts out everything important, eleven pages down to one, and even that one won't say half what he means.

Twice he actually sent them, to Amigo's PO box.

Then, in his Trans Am in a parking space on Main, revving the engine like he might take off suddenly, Amigo told him. "No more mail in the box, Patterson."

For a long time his face burned, remembering. So now he doesn't.

Amigo works on his tan. He pulls off his shirt and lies back on it across the boards of his half-built front deck. His arms are still bulky from a buff youth he has since abandoned. Or which has abandoned him. Patterson imagines they have lost bulk since he first saw them. Tattoos glisten in a sheen of sweat on his shoulders. His brushy haircut seems to have gone from black to almost copper with the sun. His black sunglasses reflect light into Patterson's eyes.

Next time, Amigo says, he will not allow his wife to give him the brushy haircut, because it only calls attention to the thin spots. This is fine with Patterson, who becomes angry and depressed thinking about Amigo's wife touching his hair.

Amigo shakes the Marlboro box. "Almost out."

Patterson borrows his motorcycle to go get more. While he's out, he'll get another twelve-pack. Save himself the second trip.

At three the next morning, Patterson pulls a blanket around himself to preserve any warmth he might muster. The low stone wall is cold against the backs of his legs. Through the trees, down the hill into town, a car rolls through the stop sign. But it's not Amigo, because both headlights point true.

It is two hours later than Amigo promised to arrive.

Patterson hikes back to his little Airstream trailer by flashlight. He knows he will not sleep. In a vacuum of suitable activities, he decides to break his hand against the trailer's metal shell. Six good blows and he is left confused as to whether he has succeeded. He sits inside and lights a cigarette left-handed. When he wakes up, the trailer smells of burned filter.

At five AM Amigo knocks.

The sun is so close to breaking that they hike without benefit of flashlight. Amigo lies on his back under a tree and looks at the stars. Amigo always looks at the stars. Lucky for him they have not entirely faded. Otherwise he might have to look down and see what he has invited. If indeed a lack of refusal qualifies as an invitation.

Patterson undoes Amigo's jeans awkwardly with his left hand.

Amigo sits up when he's done, faced away. Patterson plants a kiss on the hard knobs of his spine. Muscles tighten in Amigo's back. Patterson wonders how he could have been so stupid.

On the walk back, rays of sun cut the fog, illuminating spider webs in the scrub oaks, ornately hung with drops of moisture like rhinestone necklaces. Patterson would never admit he finds this beautiful.

At nine he has his hand x-rayed. It is disappointingly unbroken. He successfully hits the doctor up for painkillers, sleeps the day away on three of them.

The phone wakes him. It's his mother. Worse yet, Dad's on the extension. They do this every week. Still going to college in the fall? Yeah, I told you. When are you going to call Judy? She's such a nice girl. Well, soon. That's when.

He hangs up, takes back the dream.

It's been there the whole time, Patterson clutching at it, asking it to please wait.

In the dream, when they were done, he put his head on Amigo's shoulder, and they both looked at the stars, and Amigo didn't act like he had any home that needed any running off to.

Sometimes Patterson touches himself, to relieve his own pressure, but it never works. Just builds and builds, fanned by Amigo's solitary, unreturned allowances. He may come close to relieving it, if he relives the moments carefully, but in time his mind will take him back to the final, humiliating failed gesture of affection. Knowing this, Patterson stops before the sad part.

When Patterson is in love he wants the whole world to know. He wants to stop people on the street, people he's never met. He always expects to recognize it in their eyes, the same way he feels it. He never expects it to come back looking ugly and small.

Patterson gives the engine that didn't fit to Amigo. Amigo sells it and uses the money to repair the damage he did driving home from the Cayucos Tavern in his wife's car. Patterson borrows five hundred dollars from his father for a new engine. This time he talks to the guy in Morro Bay first, to make sure it will fit. Amigo's engine hoist is low on hydraulic fluid and he dings the fender of the Chevy on the installation.

"We'll bang that out next week," he says.

Patterson follows him up the Big Sur coast, pushing the tach all the way. Amigo takes thirty mile per hour curves at sixty. Then seventy. Then seventy-five. Patterson maintains the distance between their bumpers. Shoot for the apex and lean.

Coming off a hairpin by San Carpoforo, he squeezes over the centerline just as a Winnebago absorbs the sky beyond his windshield. He starts to cut, reflex, but knows the pattern of spin it will produce. He closes his eyes. He's prepared. In fact, it feels overdue. But the perceived moment of impact passes with something startlingly missing, quiet, like passing through the incorporeal body of a ghost. The Winnebago fishtails on the dirt of the cliff edge and rights itself. The driver blows his horn at Patterson. The sound seems to never end.

Amigo shoots him a thumbs up in his rearview mirror.

They stop at Gorda for coffee.

"You're in an awful hurry, Amigo."

"Only to get to the next curve, boy."

When people make babies, they make a life. Only they don't have to live it. The kid's got to live it. How do they even know he wants it? That's what Patterson would like to know. He doesn't honestly suppose people stop to think about that part.

Patterson idles at a stoplight, and a local comes to his truck window to ask if it isn't wonderful, about Amigo's wife being pregnant and all. Patterson doesn't mean to spin his tires taking off.

He finds Amigo sunning on his front deck, behind black sunglasses. Patterson is glad he can't see his eyes.

He opens his mouth to speak, but Amigo beats him to it.

"How 'bout a straight trade? Your truck for my car."

"You'd be a fool, Amigo."

"I need it, though. To haul. Maybe firewood."

"I'd be getting the good end."

"Just take care of her, boy."

Patterson allows a pause. "Goddamn it, Amigo, doesn't this mean anything to you?"

Another pause, then Amigo reaches for the Marlboro box. "I'm not sure I follow your drift, boy."

"What the hell does it mean, what we're doing?"

Amigo pulls to his feet. Patterson doesn't know whether to prepare for a blow or an embrace. A smile breaks on Amigo's face, not entirely friendly.

"What do you want me to say, Patterson? You want me to say you were good? That I never loved a woman more?"

Patterson closes his eyes, tries to let the sting pass through him and keep going. He hears Amigo twist the top off another beer. "I want you to tell me what you're thinking. I never know what you're thinking." He feels the bottlecap bounce lightly off his stomach, hears it rattle on the unfinished boards.

"I'm thinking maybe I'll take my new truck for a drive."

Patterson waits until he's gone to open his eyes. On the deck rail in front of him are the Trans Am keys. Before he can pick them up, Amigo's wife pulls into the driveway. She wrestles her big belly out from behind the wheel. Patterson feels his hands clench into fists. No part of his body seems to respond to signals. She stands on the deck in front of him, just outside the front door. She smiles. He wishes she wouldn't.

"Hi, Patterson. I never see you anymore." She watches him stare at her swollen belly. "You must be the only person in town I haven't told."

He stands immobile, sees something strange cross her face, seeming to have nothing to do with him, with anything. He jumps when she touches his wrist. His bloodless white fist goes limp. She presses his hand to her belly, and he feels the kick. He tries to pull away.

"Oh, now, don't be bashful, Patterson, all men like that."

Patterson sinks to his knees and places his ear against her. He isn't sure what he thinks he will hear.

"Run for your life," he whispers.

"What'd you say, Patterson?"

He looks up into her open face. "Nothing."

He climbs into his new Trans Am and drives the wrong way, away from home, up the coast toward San Francisco. At least, it would have seemed the wrong way before just now. He takes it easy on the curves.

LOVE IS ALWAYS RUNNING AWAY

*T*hat first night we both made love to Chloe, on the beach at Huntington, tripping our brains out on acid, I should have known the baby would turn out to be his. Only, stupid as we all were, who'd have guessed there would be one? We were all just friends at the time, too high to see that the sex would change that.

Chloe got up afterwards and ran into the freezing ocean. He rolled over and hugged me. I mean, there we were, a couple of naked guys, but you couldn't take it wrong. You just couldn't. I focused on the feeling in my chest, and the contrast of his dark skin against mine.

"Mi hermano," he said, clapping me on the back. "You are my brother."

Then Chloe got back and we sat with our bare butts in the sand, in the dark, watching the horizon bend, as if my brain was like a wide angle lens. Chloe invested us both with our totems, our spirit guides. I think she picked them out for us, but she said no. She said they just were, and she could just feel it. But I think she sized us up. Manuel's was an eagle, mine a rabbit. I think I had every right to complain, but when I did, they just gave me those looks. Like, *Gabe's doing it again.*

Manuel put his arms around both of our shoulders and told us that eagles mate in the air, flying, and when they get into it, they stop flapping their wings. And they plummet. Hopefully they finish before they hit the ground.

Chloe said if she was a girl eagle, and saw that ground looming large, she might be tempted to fake it. She was always a funny girl, Chloe. Funny more than pretty. She has one of those faces that make you happy, but you can't pin down why. At first, you almost feel like it's a favor, to fall in love with a girl like that. Boy, is that a false feeling. They always leave you in the dirt. Leave you wondering how to get that feeling back again. They always manage to turn it around on you.

Now I hear the screaming from the bottom of the stairs, the voice husky and faint, almost lost from too much use. I wonder if she has been crying all day. The neighbors will tell me soon enough.

She's soaked, of course, and her diaper weighs a ton, but mostly she's just hot, like everybody else. Everything is hot. The sidewalk, the air, or what is made to pass for it, every follicle of my hair. And this baby, this little girl, doesn't like it. Who can blame her?

I roll up the Pamper, drop it into the kitchen trash. Clean Chloe's bottom with a wet tissue. Chloita, that's what Manuel called her, when he was here. I never call her Chloita; it would be too much like summoning Manuel home.

I draw a wet washcloth along her brown belly to cool her. She smiles as trickles of water run down her sides. I smile back, and in my own smile I feel it, and it surprises me—the sharp, sweet pang of wanting to trade places with her. I hoist her, still bare, against my shoulder.

We find Chloe out on the fire escape in a long print dress and a huge, wide-brimmed hat. Why does she seek the sun if she can't take it? I wonder; besides, can this be considered sun? I squint into the discolored haze of East LA, and it glares back at me, rude and unafraid. Relentless.

Chloe raises her head to peer out from under her absurd hatbrim. "God, that silence is beautiful."

"For god's sake, Chlo, do something for her. Feed her, change her, something."

"I do everything, Gabe." A weak smile which she seems to feel will be enough. "Everything I can think of. She never stops 'til you come home."

I prop the baby more carefully on my shoulder. My arm is slippery with sweat under her bare bottom. I feel the exchange of our sweat through my shirt. I hand her off to Chloe so I can have a smoke. As soon as I do, I miss that little sweaty communion.

I take my shirt off when I'm done and lie on the fire escape, feeling the metal grate press into my back, little Chloe sleeping against my chest. A sudden gush of warm urine runs off my ribs and on down to the street. I want to ask Chloe to bring me a paper towel, but she's talking, the kind of talking from which she will never be rousted. I know she's on acid. Acid makes her talk.

"Love is always running away," she says.

"What's that got to do with the baby?"

"Nothing. It has not one thing to do with the baby. I was talking about love."

"Love is always running away," I say out loud, to see if Gabe is asleep. He is. So now I know I can watch him and talk to him, and when I look at the side of his face, I think, *Whoa. Look at it go.* I run my finger down the tip of his nose. He snores a little but that's all.

I say, "Never saw him before in my life."

Yesterday when Gabe got home from work, he got mad because the baby was crying, like that's new. She always cries until he gets home—she stops for him, not for me; it's like she's a part of him. Which is funny because any fool can see she's not his: she looks just like Manuel, dark and stubborn. Anyway, I was tripping, and Gabe knew it, only I said no I wasn't, because I got the stuff from Manuel—Gabe doesn't even know yet about Manuel's being out on parole. And I'm not too anxious to open the subject. Gabe knew I was lying because I always talk too much when I'm tripping.

He handed me the baby so he could have a smoke—he won't smoke in the house with her, or holding her—so we were out on the fire escape in all that brown haze, the sun beating like a demon, though you couldn't see it through the smog, and heat shimmering off the pavement all the way up to where we sat. I could see that heat, but I can't swear it wasn't the drug. And he combed back his hair with his fingers—it was all wet and stringy from his sweat—and he started ragging on me about how I hold her. And of course she was crying again, like she's on his side, which she is.

"Hold her like she's part of you," he said.

But, you see, she's not.

I told him about when I was little, and my mother took me over to her friend Lois' house, and I was supposed to play with her brat of a kid, but all she ever wanted to do was play Barbie dolls—what a bore—so I snuck out to where they were eating lemon cake and talking, and my mother told Lois that she's one of those women never should have had kids, and so Lois said well, why then, why did you even, and she said my daddy told her that when nature sends a baby it sends all the right feelings along with it, all those mommy kind of feelings. And she believed him, but she said it'd been ten years and there she was still waiting for it to kick in. She said she looked at me sometimes in my bed at night and wondered did I really come out of her body because there I was looking like a little stranger.

When I got done Gabe was just staring at me. Then he rubbed the butt of his cigarette on the grating under his feet and all these sparks showered down to the street and these girls walking by, from the high school, Chicana girls, going underneath, they said, "Fuckin' A, white boy, what you tryin' to do to us?"

He took off his shirt and lay out on the fire escape with her on his chest, buck naked with no diaper, and she peed all down his ribs and he didn't even care. He just looked at me and said, "Where'd you get the stuff, Chlo?"

"What stuff?" I said. "There's no stuff to get."

He said, "I wish you would wait until I get home from work, so there's someone to watch her."

But see, when he's home to watch her I don't need the stuff.

She fell asleep, right there on his belly, and he put her to bed and made dinner for us, but I couldn't eat because I never can when I'm tripping. Gabe wanted to make love. I said it's too hot. He said it's always something—if not that, then something else. Funny thing is I used to drive him crazy I loved him so much, total nuisance, but even then I could feel it running away. I think that's why, why I leaned on it so hard, and told him I loved him so much, because I was always scared I'd wake up some morning without it, just look over at him one day and think, who is this guy, and where do I know him from, and how am I supposed to love him now that I said I would?

I told him every word of that. I shouldn't have. He got the worst look on his face, like in the hospital when he went in to see the baby with Manuel, and the nurse came in and said only the father could be in there—and you see, right up to that moment none of us knew who the father would turn out to be, but any fool could see who had to leave.

That was back when he and Manuel were like brothers.

Anyway, now I think the moment is here, like I always knew it would be, because Gabe looks skinny and pale to me, and he snores and I'm not sure I know him.

And then, like he can hear the thought, he shifts around and opens his eyes and looks right into mine. I guess it's all right there to see. Because he holds out his hand to me and shakes. And introduces himself. Says he's pleased to meet me. I don't say anything back.

When I wake up she's staring at me. Kind of blank. I sense that our moment has arrived. So I shake her hand, like we're just meeting, but she rolls away. I know she's not asleep. I lie awake for awhile, hands behind my head. Wonder when she plans to tell me that Manuel is back. Even without the acid incident I would have known. It's that thing in her eyes that I can't put there. That I never could.

I always knew he'd come back for them. Because they are both rightfully his. One by her own free choice, the other by blood. It was only a matter of time.

The next day I come home from work and there he is in my living room. Sitting there waiting to see me. And god help me, all I can think is that I love him, or I did, damned if I can tell the difference now.

"Gabe," he says. He makes it sound like everything that needed saying.

"Where's Chloe? And the baby?"

"She took her to the park."

"*My* Chloe?" When I hear it, it sounds like a bad choice of phrasing. Our Chloe. Your Chloe. Nobody's Chloe.

"I made her do it. She never takes that poor kid anywhere."

"I know. I do, though."

"Yeah," he says. "I knew *you* would."

Then he commits the ultimate assault against me. He stands up. I take it as a challenge. I'm amazed how much I hate him for it. So I stand up, too, but it doesn't help much. He's a full head taller, probably outweighs me by half again. Between his size and his brownness, he makes me feel like a line drawing someone forgot to fill in. I feel faced off against him, but he doesn't seem to notice, which stands to reason. It's not the big dog that has to brace for a fight.

I say, "When did you get out?"

He looks at me kind of funny, like he just now caught the tension. "Couple weeks ago."

"How many times have you come around here since then?"

"What's your point, man?"

"Look, you want to come back here and steal from me, fine, rob me blind, there's not a goddamn thing I can do about it, but don't make me play like I like it."

Next thing I know I'm up against the bookcase, hardcover spines digging into my back, Manuel's hot breath in my face. "When the hell did I ever steal anything from you, Gabe?"

I search around in my head, but it's hard to explain. I wonder why I ever thought my sperm might have won a race against his. A rabbit can't outrun an eagle. I say, "Any minute now."

He is going to hit me. Not for anything I've just said, but for all the reasons he pretended not to bring in the door with him today. I have seen him before, about to hit someone— not me, but someone. I know the look. He is always ready to strike, and Chloe is always ready to excuse him. She says he fights with the anger of his ancestry, of his entire race. I have always meant to say, *What horseshit.* I wish she were here. I'd say it now.

I want to close my eyes, because he hits hard, and I feel it coming. But I don't. I look him in the eye. I say, "Haven't found any new ways to deal with things, have you?" Then the pause, then the kicker. "Mi hermano."

He takes a step back from me. I straighten out my shirt, the way a cat cleans itself to look casual, and as a point of pride.

"Where the fuck are you going?" he says as I open the door.

"I thought I'd go for a walk in the park."

But I've missed them somehow. Maybe they took the wrong street home while I took the wrong street here, which is as good a metaphor as any for me and Chloe. I search the park, find no Chloes that belong to me. Maybe I never owned any.

I'm stopped by a huge old Chicana woman, one I've seen before. "Where's your baby today?"

I smile and say she's with her mother. I sit at the edge of the sandbox and hear her tell her benchmate that my wife is a Chicana. This is what she gathers from seeing me with Chloita. I want to say, *She's not my wife.* I want to say, *She's white like me.* I want to say, *What woman? What baby?* I never do.

All the way home from the park my shoulder aches from the weight of this kid, but except to shift sides, I can't think how to fix it, other than to wish she was big enough to put down—only then it might be something else, something worse, like braces or running away, and then she'll probably go off and get pregnant. I can see the smile on my mother's face as this all comes back to haunt me. She believes that what goes around comes around, and unfortunately so do I.

Gabe's not there when I get back, just Manuel, sitting on the footstool by the window with his head in his hands. I'm not used to seeing him like this, so I just don't.

"Where's Gabe?" I say, and put the kid down, and the minute I do she screams. Manuel just shrugs. "You two have your talk?"

He shrugs again. "Yes and no."

I walk over to where he sits and push hard on his shoulder, so he sits up straight like I'm used to, and then I sit down on his lap, even though it's way too hot for all that. They say lovers don't feel the cold, and it might work this way, too. His cheek is right against mine, and the brushy stubble burns, but I don't mind. I sort of like that type of pain.

He says, "So what's it going to be, Chloe?" I have to ask him to say it again, because the kid is screaming so loud.

I told him before, already, but maybe he wants to hear it again, how I want to fly away somewhere and mate in the sky, over a river or a canyon, only this time I'll try to remember about birth control. There's more than one way to hit the ground. Then I look at his face and I already see it, starting to run away, but maybe this time I'll think of something before it can get too far.

We pack all my clothes into two duffle bags, and anything Gabe and I bought together I leave for Gabe, only I cheat just a little bit and put the leftovers into his old plaid suitcase, because I need it and I happen to know he never liked it anyway.

Manuel lifts the duffle bags onto both shoulders, and I drag the big suitcase, puffing and kind of listing to one side, and at the door he swings around and almost decks me with one, but I'm so much shorter than him, I duck my head and the bag just musses the top of my hair. He points with his chin to the basinette, the hotbed of that constant, shattering list of demands.

He says, "Aren't you forgetting something?"

I say, "No, I don't think so."

We lay out on the fire escape, where the air almost barely moves. Most of the night. I open my shirt and lay her down on my stomach, feeling the warm damp spot where we fit together. I want a cigarette, but I can't see how I'll get one anytime in the next eighteen years or so.

When I wake up, she's looking at me, her head up, kind of wobbly. She smiles. I run one finger over her smooth black hair.

I say, "I know you. I'd know you anywhere, little girl."

She drools on my chest. I don't mind.

RED TEXAS SKY

*C*harlie saw the moon full in the middle of the day. He crouched in the dirt beside his house, watched the other houses in his neighborhood disappear. He took off running. When he looked up the sky would be red, so he wouldn't look up.

When the sky turned red he knew the bird was coming, and he had to run, though it always caught him anyway.

Charlie heard the sound of wings beating the air but knew better than to look. The shadow enveloped him and he screamed. Talons dug into his shoulders, lifting him off the Texas soil, legs pumping uselessly. He tried to scream again as he was lifted to the blood-red sky, but the bird grasped his throat in its giant bill, choking off sound. Charlie heard the sickening crack of his neck snapping, flopping backwards.

The way it always did.

He woke up scrambling, slipped off the bed and fell with a *whump* on the wooden floorboards. On hands and knees, he scanned the ceiling. There had never been a bird in his room, not while he was awake. But there *could* be.

He sprinted down the hall to his mom's room, but he heard the voice of a stranger and did not go in.

Charlie crouched beneath an overhang of rock, watching the colors in the sky turn. He scanned the skies and hurtled to the next rock, praying to reach the cave in time.

Two more dashes and he was inside, with a safe roof, not a red sky, over his head. Charlie leaned back against the cave wall, exhausted, and allowed his eyelids to drift down.

That was when he heard it: the deafening squawk that stopped his heart and froze his blood. He opened his eyes to see the bird filling the entrance to the cave. It looked like a dinosaur. The red light of sunset refracted through its bony, paper-thin bat wings.

It moved toward him, hooked beak working the air.

Charlie padded down the hall to his mom's room and stole inside. The covers were pulled back on her side of the bed. She was nowhere around, but somebody filled Dad's side.

Charlie was about to run when the man spoke to him. He said, "You have yourself a bad dream? Climb on in."

Charlie backed up two steps. "Where's my mom?"

"Bathroom. Here she comes now. I was just telling your son here how I don't bite."

"You go on back to bed now, Charlie," she said, but the big man disagreed.

"Now, Evvie, we talked about this. Let the boy come on in. Nightmares is a funny business. Had a lot of trouble with 'em myself."

Charlie crawled in next to his mother, on the outside, away from the stranger. Quick, before she could argue.

In the morning, the stranger was still around. He sat on a high stool at the breakfast counter, drank coffee and read the sports section. He wore Dad's old bathrobe, and a blue Houston Oilers cap.

Mom put cereal and milk on the table as the stranger lit a filterless Camel.

"Charlie, this here's Ted," she said. Then she coughed and pretended to wave smoke. "I sure don't appreciate that at the breakfast table, Ted."

"Color me gone," Ted said. He scooped up his cigarettes, the ashtray, the sports section, and moved to the back patio.

Charlie poured his own milk. "I want to eat outside."

She gave him a funny look, like he'd just said, *please can I have liver for dinner tonight?* But then she shrugged and said, "Suit yourself."

Charlie set his bowl on the glass patio table. He looked out past the rows of houses, each exactly like his own, past the oil rigs to the horizon. Ted wasn't looking at him. He was reading the paper. It gave Charlie time to stare, to figure out what kind of man he was. Strong looking. Big nose, big mustache that drooped below his mouth.

He looked up. Said, "Howdy, Chuck."

"Ted, how come you call me Chuck if everyone else calls me Charlie?"

Ted folded his sports section and sailed it to the concrete. "'Cause I give you credit for being a big kid."

"I'm eight."

"My point exactly. You can call me Teddy."

"How come? How old are you?"

Teddy laughed and took a draw off his Camel. "I'm thirty-nine. Call me Teddy so you know we're even. Wouldn't want you to think I'm pretending to be a much bigger kid than you."

"Teddy? How come you wear that cap when you're not even dressed yet?"

Teddy smiled and crushed his cigarette into the glass ashtray, which was printed with the words *Greetings from Las Vegas!*

"You ask a lot of questions, don'tcha, Chuck?"

"Yeah, everybody says that." He turned back to his cereal.

"That ain't a crime though. Here, I'll show you." He took off the cap and tilted his head to show the few thin strands combed across a patch of scalp.

"My daddy was gettin' bald," Charlie said. "But he didn't wear a cap. You don't want people to know you're gettin' bald?"

"Oh, I don't know. It's not so much that I don't want 'em to know exactly. Let's just say if I have a choice between 'em knowin' I'm bald, or I'm an Oilers fan, I'd rather pump up the Oilers. Know what I mean?"

Charlie nodded. He smiled for the first time that morning.

His mom came out and kissed him goodbye. "Don't be late for school." She cut across the backyard dirt to the orange Chevy Nova and pulled away.

"Teddy? What do you have nightmares about?"

"I'll tell you in a minute." He disappeared into the kitchen and came back with a can of Coors and his cigarettes. He popped the can and lit up. "I have nightmares about a war I fought in. For a few years I had 'em all the time. Couldn't sleep more'n two hours at a stretch. Now it's not so bad."

"Vietnam?"

"Yeah. Vietnam."

"My daddy was in Vietnam."

"Yeah. Him and a lot of other guys."

"Teddy? Will you tell me one of your nightmares? Your worst one?"

Teddy sat back and blew smoke rings, nice and casual, like he hardly noticed he was doing it. "Aren't your own nightmares bad enough?"

"I'll tell you *my* worst one."

"Okay," Teddy said. "You go first."

Charlie told about the full moon out in the middle of the day, the sky turning red, and the big bird swooping down and snapping his neck like a matchstick.

Teddy told of a dream where he opens fire on a circle of Viet Cong, rakes them with his M16 and kills them, every one. Then he turns them over, and they're all little kids, some no more than ten.

"And the very last one I turn over," Teddy says, "is me."

"You? How can it be you?"

"Well, how can a giant bird snap your neck? It's a dream, right?"

Charlie said, "Oh, yeah."

"Aren't you going to be late for school?"

"Teddy? How'd you make 'em go away?"

"I didn't say they went away. I said they got better."

Charlie carried his bowl of soggy cereal inside and dumped it down the garbage disposal.

"Get me another beer while you're in there, Chuck?"

He handed Ted the can. "What made 'em get better, Teddy?"

"I guess it was when I started talkin' about it. When I was in jail, there was a group of us guys. Vietnam vets. We'd all get together on Friday evening, put chairs around in a circle, you know, talk about stuff we remembered."

"So you tell somebody what's bothering you?" Charlie leaned on Teddy's chair, staring under the brim of the cap.

"Yeah, I guess so. You know, face your fear. Now get upstairs and get ready for school. I'm gonna catch hell if your momma finds out I made you late, runnin' off at the mouth."

When Charlie came home on Thursday, his mom put out graham crackers and chocolate milk.

He set the note on the table. He couldn't quite bring himself to throw it away, but he couldn't bring himself to announce it.

She saw it when she picked up his plate. "Charlie, what's this?"

Charlie shifted his eyes to the floor and said nothing.

"Oh, dear god, not more trouble."

Charlie sat perfectly still as she opened the note and read.

She stomped to the phone with that look in her eyes. Like she could wrestle a herd of crocodiles if one happened to swim by. Like steam was about to come out of her ears if this had been a cartoon. She was a tiny woman with a way of acting bigger than her size.

She tapped her foot while she waited for an answer on the line. "Miss Yates, please." More tapping. "Miss Yates? Evelyn Higgins. Charlie's mom. Yeah, I got your note, and I don't appreciate being told I'm not doing enough." Tap tap tap. "Well, it sounded like you were. Look, Charlie's tired because he has nightmares every night. Anybody would, after what happened." She listened in silence for a few seconds, then put her hand over the mouthpiece. "Go upstairs, son," she said, "this don't concern you."

Charlie went halfway up the stairs and stopped to listen.

"My husband left us with nothing, Miss Yates. A pittance in Social Security and a big mortgage. I got to clean houses to get us by. Where do you suggest I get the money for some fancy psychologist?" Long silence. "No. That would be charity. Charlie and I don't take charity. Ain't gonna start. Look, you teach him best you can at school, and I'll do my best at home, and don't be telling me my best ain't no good!"

And she slammed the phone down hard.

"God help me," Charlie heard her say. "You left us with nothing down here. Can't you give us some kind of a hand?"

Charlie slept straight through the night, until his mom pulled the covers off what she called his lazy hide.

"Get dressed quick. We got to get you to Ada's."

Charlie found Ted downstairs eating fried eggs.

He pulled himself up to his full four foot eight. "I don't wanta go to Ada's."

His mom was on a dead run for work. "Now, that's just crazy talk. You always go to Ada's on Saturdays."

"I wanta stay here with Teddy."

"Well, that ain't up to me, that's up to Ted."

"Fine with me, hon."

She had her keys in hand, ready to break for the door. "This is my long day. I might not be home 'til eight o'clock. You sure babysittin' ain't gonna get old in about eight hours?"

"Hell, this ain't no baby."

"How do you face your fears?" Charlie asked the minute his mom was out of the driveway.

"Well. I told you how I faced mine."

"No," Charlie said. "Mine."

"Oh." Teddy lit a cigarette in the house and sat back in Daddy's old chair. "Let's see. What are you afraid of?"

"Birds."

"What else?"

"I don't know. Just birds."

Teddy tapped his ashes, scratched his head. "Ever been attacked by a bird?"

"No."

"Well, then, that's not a real fear. It's just something in a dream, pretending to be something else. Know what I mean?"

"I don't think so."

"What are you scared of that might really hurt you?"

"I'm a little scared of tractors, from when the tractor killed my dad."

Teddy said, "Bingo."

Four men in a station wagon dropped them just outside the Amarillo city limit. Ted showed his thumb to every passing car. A one-ton truck drawing a horse trailer pulled over, and a man leaned out the passenger window and asked where they were headed.

"Why, me and my friend here's goin' all the way to Lubbock."

Turned out this truck was going right through there, for anyone who didn't mind riding in the back.

Teddy settled into the truck with his back against the cab. He sat with his arms around his knees. Charlie did the same. Teddy took a Camel out of the pack rolled into his T-shirt sleeve. He wore jeans and a T-shirt, like Charlie, only Charlie had white leather tennis shoes instead of the snakeskin boots, and no Oilers cap.

Charlie watched Ted light his cigarette, shielding the flame from the wind with both hands. "When will I be old enough to smoke, Teddy?"

"Never."

"Never? I have to be old enough someday."

"Son," he said, "don't you never take up this nasty habit. Gets you by the short hairs and then you can't quit. Cuts your wind, cuts your life, and you can't do a damn thing about it."

"But you smoke."

"You're missin' the point, kid. I do lots of things, and that don't make 'em good things to do."

Charlie sat, quiet. Through the trailer window, he watched the soft-looking muzzle of a buckskin, chewing hay.

"You *can* stop," he said. "My daddy did."

"Well, Chuck, he was a better man than I am."

"You got any kids, Teddy?"

"Yeah. I got a boy."

"My size?"

"No. Hell no. Almost old enough to go out on his own. He lives with his momma in Tulsa."

"You see him, Teddy?"

"She don't let me."

Charlie peered into Ted's face, watched the tip of his Camel glow in the wind. "How come?"

"I guess she thinks I ain't a fit daddy."

"I think you'd make a good daddy, Teddy."

Teddy laughed through his nose, blowing puffs of smoke out with the laughter. "That makes one of you," he said.

At a traffic light in Lubbock, Teddy knocked on the truck's back window. He jumped the side and lifted Charlie down.

"This ain't quite our stop yet. But I need to make me a quick run into this store. Promise you won't wander off."

When Teddy got back he didn't have a bag, and he wasn't carrying anything.

"What'd you get, Teddy?" Charlie had to walk two steps, then break into a run two steps, to match Teddy's stride.

"Oh, just something."

Charlie dropped back a bit on purpose. Saw a scrap of something light blue sticking out of Teddy's back pocket. "What you got in your pocket, Teddy?"

"Oh, just something."

"Looks like a cap."

"Does it now?" Teddy put on the brakes at a stoplight, and Charlie nearly ran into the back of him. "We got almost three miles to Lloyd Turner's place. Think you can make it?"

"Sure, Teddy." Charlie broke into a run as the light changed. "I can make it."

"Good. 'Cause I ain't in no mood to wait for a bus."

They turned down Baker Road, where high chain-link fences with barbwire tops reminded him of his dad's old workplace. When he looked again, Teddy was three paces in front.

"Don't get scared yet," Teddy said over his shoulder. "We ain't even there."

"I'm not scared, Teddy. I might be a little tired."

Teddy carried him piggyback, through an open gate with a sign that said TURNER EQUIPMENT RENTAL, into the office.

Lloyd Turner was a short man who had a paunch and

smoked cigars. "Why, Ted Warren, you old son of a bitch. Ain't seen you around in years. Weren't you in jail?"

"Yeah. But I ain't there now. This here's my friend Chuck. He wants to get a close look at a tractor. I thought since we're old friends you might give me the key to one. I won't take it no further than around the yard."

Lloyd tilted his head and scowled. He motioned Ted closer with a wave of his hand. Ted set Charlie down and moved closer, but Charlie could still hear.

"You ain't had a lot to drink, have you, Ted?"

"One with breakfast, Lloyd, I swear." He held up his right hand as if he was in court.

Lloyd took a key down from a pegboard on the wall. "Number 54. It's a little Kubota."

"Good," Teddy said. "Little is good."

They stepped out into the yard. Cranes, tractors, earth movers, big monster machines at every turn. Dinosaurs.

"Teddy . . ." Charlie grabbed hold of Ted's hand.

"Okay, Chuck. I know. We're just gonna stand here awhile."

"Then what?"

"Then we're gonna walk right up to one and touch it."

"Why we gotta do that, Teddy?"

"We don't *gotta* do any of this. It was your idea to face your fear. Now, look at them machines. What're they doing?"

"Nothing."

"My point exactly. 'Cause they're just machines. They can't kill a man. A man can kill himself with a tractor but the man has to make the mistake first. Now come on."

Ted chose a big John Deere with a front end that seemed to snarl. Charlie stood within touching distance, then took a few steps back, pulling against Teddy's hand. Teddy wouldn't budge. Charlie touched the tractor, then jumped away like it had burned him.

"Come on," Teddy said. "Let's find good old number 54."

Teddy climbed up to the little Kubota and reached a hand down to Charlie, pulled him up and set him down between his thighs. "Now brace yourself, 'cause I'm gonna start it."

Teddy clutched and hit the key and the rumbly diesel engine sprang to life.

Charlie turned around to Ted and climbed him like a spooked cat. "Teddyyyy!" he wailed in Ted's ear.

"Ho, ho, whoah boy." Teddy cut the engine again. "That's just the sound the motor makes. Now, I'm going to do it a bunch more times 'til you don't jump anymore."

Nine starts later, Charlie hardly jumped. The engine warmed at a high rev as Ted drew the seat belt snug across their laps.

"It's all hydraulic!" Ted roared to be heard over the thunder of the engine. "So you got to let it warm up!"

"And then we're gonna drive on it, Teddy?"

"You bet."

Teddy took off the brake and shifted into a low gear, then rolled across the dirt lot with one arm tight across Charlie's chest. "If you keep your seat belt on," he shouted, "you won't get hurt bad, even if you roll over. See, you got your roll bar, that's this." He slapped the bar with his free hand. "That keeps it from coming down on you. And the seat belt keeps you from slipping off to where the roll bar can't save you. Did your daddy's tractor have a roll bar?"

"I think so," Charlie shouted. "But he didn't wear a seat belt."

Ted pulled the Kubota back into its original space, idled it down, lowered the front and rear implements and cut the engine. "Now, wasn't that easier than you thought?"

Charlie nodded and said nothing.

"How come you're cryin' then?"

"I peed my pants, Teddy."

"Oh, hell, is that all?" Teddy unhooked the belt and lowered Charlie down. "That ain't no big deal."

"No big deal? Everybody'll see, Teddy! I wet my pants, like a baby!"

"Babies don't know no better. It happens to grownups. If they get scared enough." Teddy jumped down, sat in the dirt with his back against one huge, knobby tire, motioned for Charlie to sit beside him. "I peed my pants once, when I was in 'Nam."

"Really? What happened, Teddy?"

"Well, it's a story I don't like to tell. I think it was just about the worst day of my whole life. But I'll tell it, if you tell me the worst thing that ever happened to you."

Charlie shook his hand: *deal.*

"My platoon was crossing this field, my buddy Rich out front. All of a sudden Rich steps on a land mine. Enemy buries it underground. When you step on it, it jumps up, about to your . . . well, like just below your waist. And then it explodes. So my friend Rich is walking in front of me, normal as you please, and next thing you know he's got no legs."

"No legs? Where did his legs go, Teddy?"

"Oh, every which way. They just went flying. Anyway, the mines're all over. God only knows where. So I pick up Rich and carry him piggyback, like I did with you. One time, just as I step down, another guy steps on a mine. I heard that bang and thought I was dead. But when I opened my eyes, somebody else was screamin'. By the time we got back to the road, I'd peed down my pants. My socks were all wet. It was a mess."

"Was Rich okay, Teddy?"

"No, Rich died. Lost too much blood. Now don't tell your momma I told you that. She'll blame me for your next nightmare. It's no story for a kid. But I know you seen some things, too."

"You mean when my daddy died."

"Your momma told me you was standin' right there."

"Almost right there. He let me go to work with him, 'cause it was summer. No school. He was on a big hill of fill dirt. Like this." Charlie tilted his hand to show the angle of the tractor. "And it goes sideways. Like it wasn't sure whether to fall. And my dad slipped under, and then it fell on him. And it slid down this pile. I ran all the way from the truck to see where he was. But he wasn't anywhere. They used one of those things to pick it up." Charlie pointed to a crane in the corner of the yard. "He was flat. Not all over, but here." He pointed to Teddy's chest. "One of his legs was all bent back like this." Charlie tried to demonstrate, but legs don't really go that way, not without a sacrifice. "And his neck was all bent back. Like . . ."

"Like it was broken?"

"Yeah. I guess. And his eyes were open. I never knew that people's eyes stay open when they're dead. My mom said being dead is like sleeping forever. But he didn't look like he was sleeping. Then everybody starts yellin', *Get the kid outta here!* And Keith grabbed holda me and carried me back to the truck."

Ted ground his cigarette butt into the dirt. Then he took the cap out of his back pocket and stuck it on Charlie's head. "You earned this. You been real brave today."

Charlie jumped up and faced Ted. "I was not brave. I was so scared I pissed myself."

Teddy lurched forward and came back in his face. "So what the hell you think brave is, boy? Huh? You think it's when you're not scared? Well, I got news for you. When you're the most scared ever, and you get through, wet pants and all, then that's the bravest you ever been."

"Oh." Charlie tried to brush off the soil, stuck in a layer on the seat of his wet jeans. "Teddy? How old were you? That day in Vietnam?"

"Eighteen."

"Oh. You were big."

Teddy laughed bitterly. "Yeah, that's what I thought, too."

Teddy took off his big T-shirt at the Tidi-Wash Laundromat and gave it to Charlie to wear. It fit him like a tent, coming down below his knees. Charlie peeled off his wet jeans and jockeys from underneath.

Teddy had a big chest with an amazing amount of hair. He even had hair on his back. He had bulgy arm muscles, and a stomach that rode over his belt. And tattoos. Lots of them. A naked lady, and a little mouse. A banner with a name too faded to read. A Tasmanian Devil. One that just said, *Ted.*

He bought a fifty-cent box of detergent from the machine on the wall, poured the whole thing into the washer and started it turning.

Charlie put his socks and shoes back on, and Teddy grabbed him by the wrist and said, "Come on."

"Where we goin', Teddy?"

"To church."

"Church? But Teddy, it's not even Sunday."

"So? Who told you it had to be Sunday? Come on."

Charlie held his ground, glued to the laundromat chair. "Are people gonna laugh at me, Teddy? Like I'm wearin' a dress?"

Teddy looked him over. "No, if I was to see you on the street, I'd figure you just came from a swim."

"Oh. Well, that's okay, then."

No sooner was Charlie out the door than he realized he was tired. He asked Teddy to carry him piggyback.

"Why we goin' to church, Teddy?"

"Never hurts to go to church."

"Oh."

When Teddy carried him up the church steps and through the door, Charlie saw they were the only ones there. Teddy said it was better that way. He said it would be easier to get god's attention without all those people talking at once.

Charlie looked around the place like it might contain a giant bird. It wasn't like the chapel in Charlie's neighborhood. This was a big place, ceiling higher than both floors of his own house, banks of stained glass windows, two at a time on each wall, two behind the altar, and the altar behind an iron gate.

Teddy set him down in the front pew.

"What am I supposed to pray for, Teddy?"

"Well, Chuck, no man can tell another man what to pray for. But I suggest you keep to somethin' you might get."

"Can I say I'm mad at my dad for not wearin' a seat belt?"

"You can say whatever's true."

"Can I ask why he didn't?"

"Yeah, but a big voice ain't gonna come out of the sky. Maybe the answer'll come later, some other way."

"But he always answers?"

"Well, kid, there's two schools of thought on that. Maybe your daddy just forgot. Maybe he was so all-fired used to going without the belt he convinced himself no bad could come of it. I made a mistake like that."

Charlie held his hands in the prayer position, turned to look at Ted, head still bowed. "You're not dead."

"No. I didn't kill myself with this mistake, I killed somebody else. Comin' out of a bar, two AM, had a few beers in me, went to drive home, which anybody'll tell you not to do. Just like anybody'll tell you to wear your seat belt on a tractor. But I'd done it and done it, and nothing ever seemed to go wrong. Guess I started thinkin' nothing ever would."

Charlie stared, eyes big and round. "Who'd you kill, Teddy?"

"Oh, it was this elderly lady. I came over the divider and hit her head on. I wasn't hurt bad, but she died."

"Was everybody mad at you?"

Teddy raised his eyes to the ceiling as if god would corroborate. "That don't hardly say it, boy. I spent four years in the penitentiary."

"But you didn't do it on purpose."

"No. But I did it. Your daddy didn't kill himself on purpose, but he's just as dead, now isn't he?"

Charlie took a few deep breaths and turned back to his work. "Am I supposed to pray out loud?"

"Doesn' matter."

"Am I supposed to say what I prayed for?"

"Doesn' matter."

"I'm all done, Teddy," he said a few minutes later.

"Good. Let's go see if your pants are, too."

Charlie picked the window seat and Teddy let him have it. He looked beyond the Greyhound window, across the flat Texas landscape. Twenty minutes out of Lubbock he turned to Ted and broke the silence.

"I didn't only pray for the nightmares to stop, Teddy. I prayed you won't go."

Ted sucked in a deep breath. "Well, that's real nice now, son. Only it's a subject where no one can make you no guarantees. It's your momma's house. I can only stay long as we're gettin' on good. Funny thing about a man and a woman gettin' on. I wonder if the good lord himself understands it."

Charlie nodded, and his eyes drifted back to the scenery. "My mom says I'll understand that stuff when I'm older."

He looked back to Ted, who smiled like he shared a good private joke with himself. "I'd like to be some assurance to you, son, but I'm older, and I don't understand."

Teddy changed the subject then. Explained how Warren Moon was the best quarterback in the NFL, and why, and how Houston would come out on top of the AFC this season, finally.

Charlie fell asleep partway through. Teddy had to lug him home in a fireman's carry, all the way from the bus station to a plenty unhappy mom.

For that one night there were no dreams. No birds.

He would wake in the morning and hope for the same again, knowing it's a subject where nobody can make you no guarantees.

SAM WILL REMIND ME

*I*t isn't hard to single out Sam's widow. She's the one everybody hugs. Other than that I don't know her; I don't know anybody in this service—or for that matter, this town. I feel like a cheat, like I slipped in, even though we're outdoors on the beach, even though the paper says all are welcome. I feel guilty, even though Sam was not my lover. I have sand in my shoes, and the wind is cold under my dress.

Morro Rock stands behind us in the darkness. I hate to look, but it's there, a slate ghost. Across the harbor the lights of Morro Bay shimmer on the hill, beautiful but false, a cheap, man-made imitation of moonlight shimmering on water. Tears come when I think of moonlight on water. Funny, because I never cry.

Morro Rock is the reason I moved here, ran here, am visiting, hiding, whatever. A guy on the program in LA, an atheist, used the Rock as his higher power for thirteen years. Successfully. So far my impression is that it's worth less to me; still, it's spooky that Sam's memorial is here at the foot of it. Whose side is this power supposed to be on?

A man reads from the Bible, then the Tao Te Ching—the former, I assume, for us, the latter for Sam. I wonder: *is he here*? Will he still look after me? I saw him in a dream last night; he looked like a clear blue flame, but it was Sam all right.

She walks to me. I freeze in fear, freeze over a flight response that might send me off if my feet weren't planted and my brain wasn't mush. My hands shake, but when don't they?

She tilts her head and looks into my eyes. If she wasn't so polite she'd ask, *Who are you*?

I say, "I'm new in this town. I don't know anybody. I only knew Sam a little, but he . . ." What? What was I going to say? He loved me and let me love him and he didn't try to fuck me, but he let me play out my disease on him, make him my world, and all in just a couple of weeks?

I try to say he was friendly, but the words make me cry. I never cry, but she doesn't know that. For all she knows I cry during *Bonanza*, and *Little House on the Prairie*. The evening news.

I'm blowing it. I always do.

She takes me in her arms, calls me a beautiful girl, and she's not quick to let go. She gives me time to fall in love with her first. I don't need much time.

People hug her and wander to their cars, and then it's just us, and a long breakwater to our right, and that foghorn that chills me, takes me back to the night I came down here with Sam, before we figured out we couldn't be alone like that.

I can't move away from her. I'll never see her again. She doesn't have a fixed address; they lived on a wooden boat in the marina. I'm looking at her, she's looking back, but we don't move closer. That damned foghorn keeps cutting at me.

After a while she takes three steps in.

"Were you Sam's lover?"

"Sam didn't have a lover. He never cheated on you."

She tilts her head again. Her hair is mostly gray but also a little blonde, her face soft, like someone who would never hurt me. She's about twice my age.

"How do you know that?"

"He told me."

"Strange thing to tell someone you only know a little."

"Maybe."

"He was in love with you, though. Right?"

Oddly, I had not considered that. He was my angel. Does that have anything to do with love? We desperately longed to bed each other, but that definitely doesn't. This much I know.

"He was in love with somebody. I figured it must be you."

"Maybe."

"Were you in love with him?"

What if I say I don't know? I can't talk to normal people. I think a normal person knows if they're in love or not, but I can't state this for a fact.

"Sam was not my lover."

"Thank god."

I turn and look at the slate ghost.

One day Sam picked me up outside the shop, just after work, on his baby, his true love, his steel-gray, futuristic Honda Hawk.

"Long ride or short ride?"

"Long ride."

He turned north on the highway, opened up the throttle, and I felt a rush, the kind I used to chase in the form of sex and evade in the form of Valium, and it struck me funny for the first time. I'm always chasing the same feeling I'm trying to kill. I'd been off Valium three weeks by then, sex two, and I wondered if Sam could feel my hands shake through his leather jacket.

North of San Simeon—that's Big Sur country, and the highway twists and turns and climbs and hairpins and switches back, and I wasn't sure about the leaning thing. I let it be a slow dance. I let him lead.

The higher we got, the farther the ocean stretched out, the farther away I went in my head. I thought he'd come to take me away from myself. I thought we'd never turn around.

We stopped in a place called Gorda. A store, a gas pump, and a restaurant.

We ate calamari. I tried to think how to explain that sex, to me, would be like a martini to a dry alcoholic. There must be a way to say, *If you really care, you won't*, but I never found it. I small-talked, hinted at a problem, stomped it to death, actually, made it painfully clear that I was one sick puppy, but never said it straight out.

After dinner we crossed the highway to the cliff, he stood behind me, and we watched moonlight shimmer on the water, all interconnected like a knight's silver mail. He was not quite touching me, but I could feel him, like a spark that jumps a gap. Warning signs went off in my head, but I liked dancing just at the edge of a flame. I thought I could get out without burns, even though I never had before.

He asked me if I wanted his jacket. He said, "You're shaking."

"It's the Valium withdrawal. It could go on for months."

He slid one arm around my waist, and I pulled a breath that wouldn't push out again. He wasn't tall, about my height, and his chin rested on my shoulder. My throat was too tight to talk. I wanted to say, *Please don't*, because it was too late, if he moved I'd move with him.

After awhile he said, "We better go back before we do something we'll regret."

Before we got on the bike I asked if I'd been a good passenger on the way up. If I could do anything better.

"Maybe be there more. Not such a light touch. Let me know you're there."

I wasn't sure if that had any direct bearing on his ability to drive, but he didn't say it in a coy way, like he just wanted the contact. So I was there.

Hold him as tight as you'd hold him in bed, I tried not to think, but it kept coming back. The way was mostly downhill, which slid me forward against him, and I can't be that close to a man and entertain a sexual thought that he can't hear and feel.

He dropped me home, didn't ask to come in.

My jeans felt surprisingly wet when I peeled them off, my room too hot. I went right to bed but sleep never came.

The only other time we were alone was out at the end of the Rock, where the ocean swelled underneath us like the breath of something living. In the dark.

I kept looking at that whirlpool of power, never at Sam, and so was able to tell him some things, and not tell him others. Some things will die with me—not soon, I hope. I will not give them up, not to Sam, my sponsor, my therapist, not to my god, if I ever find one.

He said he'd been married twenty-two years, the time I've been alive, if you call it that, and had never betrayed his wife.

I said, "Don't fuck it up now."

I could feel his bare arm inches from mine, and when he moved even slightly it changed my pulse and breathing, as though he moved against me, or inside me. He said I was the first time he wanted to, really would have, and it was interesting that the best favor he could do me was to resist, almost like something was taking care of us. I looked at the Rock, rising like a slate ghost into the fog, but it just looked like a rock. I'd given up on it.

And besides, we almost did.

He walked me to my car, and stood there trying not to smile, and I reached out to kiss his cheek and almost fell in, like a whirlpool that takes away your choice of direction until there's nowhere to go but down.

He held my shoulders and said, "Whoa." No man had ever said that to me before. "You almost forgot."

No, I didn't forget; I just didn't care.

He said, "I'll remind you."

Two days later, at the post office, mailing a letter to my sponsor, I looked up and saw him through the glass. Walking.

I pressed my hand against the window. He trailed his finger along the outside of the glass, and when we crossed I felt a rush of chemical-based emotion, as though he had pinned me into a corner, cupped his hands on my breasts, parted my lips with his tongue. I thought, *The whole electromagnetic field of the Earth is against us, it will pull until we're too tired to hold on.* It's only a matter of time.

The following Monday I read the paper and Sam was dead. And nobody to blame. Because the man who drove the car that took him wasn't drunk, or reckless, or speeding, except that he was passing on a two-lane stretch of Highway 1, and no charges had been filed. He just didn't see my Sam, a steel-gray ghost whose life went for nothing more important than an oversight, a trick of the light, a blind spot.

Gone.

We lean on the railing of Sam's old wooden boat, her home. Tied in a slip in the marina, watching a thin crescent of indistinct yellow moon set on the western horizon. I know it marks the end of something, but not what.

She says, "Do you know why I asked you here?"

I not only don't know why, I didn't know that she had, only that we had begun walking down the Embarcadero together, and this is where we ended up. Now that I consider motives, I can only think that she might want to kill me, but that's not what I see in her eyes. Actually I don't know what I see in her eyes, I can't read it, but it's not murder. This much I know.

"No. I don't."

"Because I don't want to be alone."

"No family? Friends?"

"None that would be any help."

No one has suggested I might be of help before. I'm not sure how to take it.

"You don't even know me."

"Yes, I do. You're the girl Sam was in love with."

If she knew half of what I've been through she'd give me credit for womanhood. I shift around a little. I'm never good with words, except in my own head.

"I think it was just . . . well, you know." She doesn't seem to. "That time in a man's life when he wants to know a young woman can still want him."

"A young beautiful woman."

"I wouldn't say that."

"And thin."

Yeah. Actually, too thin. Or I will be if I don't watch it. Since kicking Valium and sex there's the eating thing again.

"I only met him three weeks ago."

"It doesn't take long to fall in love."

I watch her face in profile, her hair parting and blowing across her eyes. Yeah. Tell me. "Do you hate me?"

"I'm trying really hard. But no."

"Doesn't it help that I never touched him?"

"No. It would almost be better if it had been all sex. Meaningless. I hate that he cared about you."

I take a deep breath and squeeze my eyes shut in the closest I will come to prayer. "Do you want me to leave?"

"No."

In her voice I hear the desperation I feel, and I breathe again. And look at her again. There's a thin lifeline between us, and it's all we have. Three hours ago I didn't know her. My life moves too fast—I'm always fighting motion sickness. I feel the sway of the harbor swell, a kind of rolling instability. I always feel that lack of foundation, only less realistic.

I open my mouth to state something, some mitigating circumstance. To enter some new plea.

She touches her fingers to my lips. "Don't talk now."

She descends into the hold and comes up with a bottle of brandy. No glasses. She unscrews the top and throws it overboard. After a long swallow she offers the bottle to me.

Technically, trying to recover from drugs and all, I shouldn't. Alcohol is considered a drug, and although it's not the one that hamstrung me, I'm blowing my time on the program as I take the bottle. I press my lips where hers just were, tilt my head back. It burns going down, and I like it.

The moon is gone, so is the brandy, and it's been awhile since anybody's said a word.

"So what are you going to do now?"

She bursts into serious tears, the kind that terrify me, a broken water pipe, all at once with no way to shut it off. I never allow myself that luxury. I just know I would never stop.

"I'm sorry. I never should have opened my mouth. I'm sorry."

I feel her arms around my neck, and although paralyzed I try to hold her saying, "Shhhh. Shhhh." But my theory is correct. The shutoff is broken. I hold her until the violent sobs become hiccups and hitches. Forever. Then I help her down into the hold.

"You need to put on some warm pajamas and get under the covers. That's what I would do."

She startles me by grabbing hold of my collar.

"No. I don't want to go to bed. You'll leave."

"No. I won't. I'll stay."

"Even if I go to sleep?"

"Yes, I promise."

She lets go of me, reluctantly, and pulls a flannel nightgown out of a small chest of drawers. And undresses. This is awkward. My eyes can't decide where to rest. I glance at her body. It looks like warm comfort, like a hot bath, or a hot drink, or a wool blanket on a cold night. Then I look away, ashamed.

She lies on the bed, and I lie down with her, on our sides, facing, and I realize this was Sam's bed, three days ago. And I realize that without her I would have nowhere to go, except to draw a double lungful of water and sink. And then I realize I don't know this woman's name, and she doesn't know mine, and it doesn't matter, anyway. And I wish I hadn't had the brandy, because it is a drug. I feel it. It's that out of control sensation, and things happen. They just happen.

And through this dust devil of thoughts I feel that the thread that holds us is thin, and maybe it's breaking, even though I've felt this hundreds of times before and somehow, regrettably, lived to tell of it.

I kiss her on the mouth. A gentle kiss, tentative, but not brief. I cup her face in my hand, and her lips part, just slightly, and as I press my tongue between them, I notice that she doesn't exactly kiss me back, but she has plenty of room to retreat, which she also doesn't.

I touch just above her knee, where flannel yields to skin, and slide up her thigh, her nightgown rising and bunching above my hand. She takes my wrist, doesn't displace it, but holds it too hard, somewhere between stubborn and violent. Pain replaces my circulation.

I pull my hand back. I pull both hands back, a surrender.

"Okay. I'm sorry."

"Go to sleep now." She rolls away from me.

"Okay. I'm sorry."

My hands to myself, I press my forehead between her shoulder blades. My tears must leave a wet spot on the back of her nightgown, but it's never mentioned.

In the morning she is nowhere at all. I sit out on the deck, thinking she'll be back, thinking I'll outwait her. But then I climb off the boat and stumble down the dock because she must not want to see me. Anyway, that will sound good on the record . . . . Actually I am feeling a little under it with last night's drunk, and the only solution seems to be to do it again.

I sit on the patio of a restaurant on the embarcadero, looking out to the harbor, the Rock, the Useless Rock, and eat a roast beef sandwich and drink four beers. This takes time. Enough to tell the Rock what a disappointment it's been, enough to realize I'm at least as scared of her as she is of me.

I walk two miles out of my way to buy roses. Red, I say, but no, that's for love, isn't it? Yellow, isn't that friendship? Isn't friendship what I'm supposedly espousing here? I wouldn't know. I'm drunk again, and besides, I never listen when I talk.

I write out a card, but I don't use her name because I don't know it, and I don't sign mine because she won't recognize it. I write what's important. "I'm sorry."

I carry them back to the slip, which is empty. No matter how many times I check to see that it's the right slip, it always is. And it's always empty.

I sit on the edge, dangle my feet over the surface of the shiny harbor. One by one, I drop yellow roses into the water, and as I do, I say, "Goodbye, Sam. Goodbye, Sam's Widow. Goodbye, Sam. Goodbye, Sam's Widow," until they are gone. I watch them drift against the hulls of other boats, that have not sailed away. And I do not feel that I have drowned. And I do not feel that Sam is gone. Sam's Widow, yes. But not Sam.

"I have a friend on the other side," I tell the Rock, "which may not be much, but it's better than you." I walk back to my room and light a candle, and stare at the flame for the longest time. It isn't clear blue, and it isn't Sam, but something is. He is here somewhere.

I ask him what I'm supposed to do now.

One of us answers. I can't swear it isn't me. But in any case, it says something like this: The trick is not finding someone who will tell me. The trick is knowing. I am supposed to know.

So I call my sponsor. Not to ask her what to do, but to tell her that I know.

She says, "So. You're not dead yet."

I say, "No. Not yet."

"But you had a little slip."

"No. Not a little one."

"But it's over now."

"How do I know?"

"If you want it to be over, it's over."

"It is, then."

"And you're coming home."

"Yeah. I'm coming home."

"Good."

I blow out the candle and pack my things.

At 3:10 AM on an October morning, 1987, Howard walked into a police precinct house in Manhattan. He'd looked in the telephone book before leaving Richard Bolt's apartment, and this was the closest one. The lights inside made him blink in a conspicuous way, or at least in a way he imagined to be conspicuous.

The uniformed officer at the front desk did not initially look up. He was eating a sandwich and reading yesterday's *Daily News*. Howard failed to respect him immediately. He was too fat, and he did not take his job seriously. A man should take something seriously, Howard felt, his job, himself. Ideally both. He cleared his throat.

"Yeah?" Still no eye contact.

"My name is Howard Sullivan."

"And?"

"I've come to turn myself in."

The officer set his sandwich down on its sheet of white butcher paper and squinted at Howard's face. "Howard Sullivan? Do we have a warrant for your arrest?"

"Not yet, no."

Howard heard the man suck in air, a sigh in reverse. "Just have a seat on that bench. I'll get a detective to come take a statement."

The bench felt cold on the backs of Howard's thighs; he tried to blink less often. The fat man picked up the phone, spun his chair away before speaking. Howard heard most of his words anyway. *Yeah, that's what he says. No, I didn't ask. Looks like a wacko.* Then, spinning back, drawing politeness from nowhere, "Detective Rennick will be right with you."

A long, cold, bright ten minutes.

Detective Rennick stood at the mouth of the hallway. "Follow me, please." Howard followed him through an open doorway, a swinging wooden gate, into a sea of desks, half occupied. A scattering of ringing phones. "Have a seat, Mr.—"

"Sullivan."

Rennick had a nose that spilled over too much of the landscape of his face, a topographical map gone awry. And a bad haircut. He fiddled briefly with his computer keyboard, then requested a string of details. Howard's address, phone, date of birth. Howard wondered why Rennick would need his home address when he would not be returning home.

"Now. Mr. Sullivan. You say you've committed a crime."

"Killed a man, yes."

"When did this *alleged* killing take place?"

Howard blinked at his watch. "Twenty-two minutes ago."

"Location?"

"Two two seven seven Second Avenue."

"The victim? Is his identity known to you?"

"His name is Richard Bolt. Was. I threw him off the roof of his apartment building."

Rennick examined Howard carefully. Howard knew Rennick assumed he was insane. Everyone did. Something about Howard's eyes. Women crossed the street before passing, convenience store clerks watched him with a hand under the counter or in a half-open drawer.

"And are you sure that Mr. Bolt died as a result of this fall?"

"It's a twenty-storey building. Shouldn't you be reading me my rights? Not to tell you how to do your job."

"It's like this, Mr. Sullivan. To arrest you, I need to establish that a murder has taken place. That would involve a body. No one has called in to report a body in the street on Second Avenue. But I suppose I'll have to send someone over." He trudged through this speech wearily, as though Howard had dirtied something he'd spent much time and effort to clean.

"Why is it," Howard asked, "that when a man comes in to confess to a killing you people make the assumption that he has done no such thing?"

"Because, in my sixteen years at this desk, Mr. Sullivan, the following pattern has emerged. Those who come in and admit to a crime have not usually committed one. Those who have committed a crime do not usually come in and admit it."

"Yes," Howard said. "I am the exception to almost every rule."

It is a Friday afternoon in 1994. Payday at Howard's new job at the dry cleaners. Howard's first payday in six and a half years. Having cashed his check on the way home, Howard stands in the lobby of his new apartment building with a mattress and a worn but useful wool blanket hand-carried from the Salvation Army store.

Howard presses the elevator button three times. Beside him stands a small, young Puerto Rican woman and her two children, a girl of about six, a boy younger. He hears a sound. Glancing over, he sees that the woman has begun to cry.

She points to a small handwritten sign that announces the elevator is out of order.

"I'm sorry," she says, wiping away tears the way she might erase a penciled mistake. "Stupid thing to get emotional about. But I live on the twentieth floor."

Howard is surprised that the woman spoke to him. Strange women do not speak to him. "Actually," he says, "so do I."

"Tough piece of luck." Indicating the mattress.

"I've had worse. It's only a twin."

Howard is unafraid of stairs. Every day for the last five days he has run up and down the twenty floors twice before work. More challenging than running on the street or in the park.

"Well, come on, kids," she says.

Howard balances the mattress on his head. It flops down to block his vision, but he only needs to see the stairs below his feet. He doesn't need to see the woman who climbs with him, and more to the point, she doesn't need to see him.

They have not even reached the third floor when the boy begins to whine. He is tired. A little farther, his mother says, but it is not a little farther. It is seven times farther, and the boy will not make the climb. His whining escalates to crying, and the woman's tears of frustration seem less incomprehensible to Howard.

Howard allows the mattress and blanket to fall onto the stairs behind him. Everyone looks surprised.

"How about a ride, then?" The boy is not afraid of him. Most children are afraid of him, wounding him with looks usually reserved for big, mean dogs. Howard crouches down on the stairs, and the boy climbs onto his back and wraps his arms around Howard's neck.

The woman argues in a tone that begs him not to listen to her argument. "But—your mattress."

"I'll come back for it."

"He's a nice man," she tells the boy. "Isn't he, Rico?"

The boy's breath is warm on Howard's ear. "I'll say."

"I don't want to walk, either." The girl.

"Reina!"

"But I'm tired. Rico gets to ride."

Howard swings her up to his hip. They climb in silence, two floors. Howard feels their hearts beat against his ribs. Then the girl says, "I like him, Momma."

"We all do, honey."

When the woman stops to rest, Howard pretends he needs to rest, too, because she will want her children in full view.

Rico says, "Are you tired, Mister?"

Howard says, "Only a little."

He returns her children to her in front of her apartment door. She lives in 20K, Howard in 20J next door.

"You just moved in last week, didn't you?"

"Yes. That's right."

"I can't thank you enough."

She has, though. She has told her children that he is a nice man. "I didn't mind."

He goes back downstairs for his mattress.

The following day he buys a weight bench with two bars and three hundred pounds of weights. Secondhand. He brings them home in a cab; now he cannot afford dinner.

The elevator is working.

He sets up the weights, two hundred pounds to bench-press, seventy-five to curl. He does not use the clips that hold the weights onto the bar. Because he knows enough to keep them level, and because he is alone. Bench-pressing with no one to spot him, the weights must remain free.

He lies on his back with his knees up, pressing the two hundred pounds in sets of twenty-five. A torn flap of vinyl irritates his back. He will have to buy tape to repair it. While he is lifting, nothing must distract him.

On the third set, the sound of a fight filters through the thin wall from the neighboring apartment. A one-sided fight. Only the man is yelling. The words are blessedly muffled. Then Howard realizes they are in Spanish. At first he is re-lieved, later he believes he knows what they mean anyway.

Fourth set, the woman's crying becomes a thin wail. Howard's arm muscles tremble. Fifth set, no yelling, only the wail. Howard wants to tell her not to waste it like that. All that power, all that emotion, dissipating like a smoky smol-der with no flame. Like evaporation. When it could be made to serve.

Sixth set. Rep fourteen. Howard has ignored his body's sig-nal to quit. He tries to push the bar off his chest one final time. For the first time in his adult life he will abandon a set unfinished. But the bar won't move. Muscles like jelly; they fail. He endures the weight on his chest a moment, then tips the bar. Half the weights fall off onto the bare wood floor; a loud report. The bar seesaws, the rest of the weights fall.

The crying stops suddenly. Someone below bangs on the ceiling—Howard's floor—he guesses with a broom handle.

He strips off his clothing and lies naked on the bare mat-tress in the dark. The wool blanket scratches.

Howard sits bolt upright in bed. Instantaneous sweat. He knows no one. Why would someone knock on his door?

"Who is it?"

"Rosa. From next door."

He pulls on his pants. But his shirt is wet. He's rinsed it out by hand, it's hanging in the bathroom. He wraps the blanket around his shoulders. Opens the door.

As it swings, the cold wash of fear. Her face will be black, swollen. She will be crying. And bleeding. She has come for help. Allison all over again.

But Rosa is smiling. She has a gift, a piece of cake on a paper plate. Chocolate, with chocolate frosting.

"I made this from scratch. I thought you might like some. You know. Just a little way to say thank you." She has dark eyes, almond shaped; black bangs fall across them.

"Thank you," Howard says. He takes the plate, and the blanket falls off one shoulder. He wishes he had never gotten the tattoos. He realizes he does not own a fork. Or a napkin. He knows he should invite her in, but he is ashamed. The mattress and weight bench are all he owns.

"Where did you live before?"

Howard notices that it did not take her long to stumble onto the wrong question. "Not in town. I just moved back to town."

"From where?"

He hesitates. In case there is a truth that is not the whole truth. "Attica." He would not even consider a lie.

"Oh. Where the prison is. I'd be scared to live in Attica."

"I was scared. Living there."

"How long were you there?"

"Six and a half years."

"You couldn't have been too scared."

"I was, though. Sometimes things keep you from moving. Even if you want to." Her resolve to chat wavers, he feels it. It's awkward in the doorway, where he cannot say come in. She is about to turn for home. "Does he hit you?"

Her eyes grow wide and search him. He wants to be invisible, because he still believes if she looks closely enough she'll see what everyone else sees. If only he hadn't asked. "No. He just yells. He gets mad, you know? Frustrated. Like we all do."

"When *you* get frustrated you cry. You don't scream at anybody."

"I have to go."

"I'm sorry. That was none of my business."

"It's okay." Three steps back to her own door.

"Thanks for the cake."

"Of course. It's okay."

Now the hall is empty, and Howard retreats.

He takes his pants off again, sits up in bed. Eats cake with his fingers. When he's done he washes his hands and face at the bathroom sink. Makes a mental note to buy a towel.

Howard runs up and down the twenty flights three times; makes himself late for work. He has two shirts now, so he changes to the clean one, and stands at the elevator to wait.

Ding. It arrives. The doors open. He steps on, and hears her call to please hold the door. He puts his hand between the rapidly closing sections. They hit with a soft thump and jerk open again.

Rosa steps in. He should never have asked a personal question. Now she is too embarrassed to talk to him, and he enjoyed that luxury before he spoiled it. They both stare at the lighted display of floors. Sixteen. Fifteen. Fourteen.

In the periphery of his vision, he sees Rosa turn to glance at the side of his face. "He used to hit me."

"I never should have asked that. I hope you'll forgive me."

"No, it's okay. You always wonder what the neighbors are thinking. Couple months ago I took the kids and went back to my mother's. And I wouldn't come home until he promised never to do it again. He hasn't raised a hand to me since."

He'll do it again. Howard almost says it, but doesn't. Not because it isn't his business, although it isn't. She knows, and she knows he knows. Everybody knows. Stop ten strangers on the street, ask if he'll do it again. They all know.

Six. Five. Four. "Thank you for caring, but I'm okay."

Before the door opens he feels her hand on the sleeve of his clean shirt. She stands on her toes and briefly kisses his cheek. Hurries off without looking back. Howard reaches a hand up to his cheek. The feeling mixes and curdles and fights with the dread.

Not again.

I'll move, he thinks.

He has to run all the way to work to be on time. The running keeps his mind free of thoughts. It keeps him from knowing that he will not move. That it is already too late for that.

Howard is running a fever. But he has been to work all the same. He has worked just as hard.

He slips into the elevator beside a small man. A dark and angry man. Proud. Well, pride crosses a line and then it is angry. There is always something to fuck with a man's pride. Howard punches twenty. The elevator begins to climb.

He does not turn to look at the man, but reads him by feel, by the energy that pours off him in waves. He wonders if the man knows how much he reveals.

Howard notices that the man did not select a floor. He hopes this is an oversight. He hopes the man is not going to twenty. That he is not who Howard thinks he is. Wasted hope, because he knows.

They step off together on the twentieth floor. Stand at their doors, rattling for keys. Howard feels dizzy. He is sick, really sick. The kind of sick he hates. The kind that cannot be overcome by will. He allows himself to stare briefly at the man, whose eyes meet and challenge his immediately.

"What the hell are you looking at?"

"Nothing much."

The man steps inside his apartment; either does not acknowledge or does not realize that he has been insulted.

When he hears that the children have gone to school, the man to work, he uses Rosa's phone to call in sick.

Then he thanks her, moves to the door. Tries not to say more. The next thing Howard says will be, *If he ever does. If you even think. You call me. You pound on the wall. You come to me. I'll put a stop to it.*

"Feel better," she says when he lets himself out.

She knocks later that morning. She holds a steaming plastic bowl. He invites her in, because the place has improved. He has a radio now. Eating utensils. A chair. Towels.

She looks around. "You sure don't have many of the comforts of home here. I made chicken soup."

"That's so nice."

"What if you get really sick?"

"I think I am really sick."

"Who will come take care of you?"

"Not a soul."

"Not even a girlfriend?"

Howard smiles and puts himself back to bed. "Do I look like a man who would have a girlfriend?"

"Well, sure. Why wouldn't you?" She doesn't sound sure. Howard doesn't answer. "Well, you could . . ." His eyes come up to her face, which has grown more beautiful. I could what? "You know. Kind of soften the look a little. Grow your hair out, maybe. Might look friendlier."

Howard has taken to shaving his head along with his face, because it saves buying shampoo. Then he lets it all grow out into five o'clock shadow for a few days.

"It's the eyes, though."

"I think you exercise too hard. I think that's why you got sick. If you slowed down a little, you'd put on some weight. You know, not look so—" She means even when he's healthy he looks sick. He would sooner curtail his breathing. "You must have had a girlfriend sometime."

"Once. But it was a long time ago. There's a spoon in that drawer." He points, and she finds it. And brings it. And he starts on the soup. Immediately, it warms something, fills something. A spot that was hollow. He is a starving man.

"So, if you had a girlfriend once you can have one again."

Howard shakes his head. "She dumped me."

"Well, that happens to everybody. You go out and try again."

No, *you* go out and try again. She dumped me. I was loving her and she came and said never mind. It's not worth the trouble anymore. *You* go out and try again. "You're stronger than I am."

She laughs, but looks to see if he is kidding. He's not. "Nobody's stronger than you."

"Everybody's stronger than me. Especially you. Every day that you stay with him you take a chance of getting hurt."

She sits down beside his mattress. "Who else would have me?"

"Anybody would. I would."

It was a short sit. She is on her feet, looking out the window. "It's hard to meet somebody when you have kids."

"I like your kids."

"Well. I should go."

Her hand on the knob. Frozen. She turns slowly, not all the way. Still half facing the door. "If you get really sick I'll take care of you."

"I am really sick."

"I'll take care of you."

Now she is gone.

After dinner she brings a plate to Howard, but doesn't stay long. I've scared her away, he thinks. He leaves the plate untouched. The chicken soup did not stay down, he has no reason to think he'll do better now.

The yelling begins. Howard wishes he had learned more Spanish when he had the opportunity. He hopes it is not about him, but likely it is.

He stands, wobbly, and moves to the thin wall, which feels cold against his ear. Wincing, and braced. If he hears the sound of a blow, he thinks he'll go right through the wall. He knows he probably can't, even healthy, but it's building so strongly in him. He might.

He never hears it.

She brings breakfast but he still hasn't eaten his dinner.

"Is he mad that you're coming over here?"

Her face startled, her words calm. "It doesn't matter."

"Don't do it if it's going to make trouble."

"Hey. I said I was going to take care of you."

"You have no idea what this means to me." He holds her arm, which seems to unnerve her.

"It's nothing. It's not a big deal."

But it is. To him.

She looks in on Howard until he is back on his feet, but mostly while the man is gone to work.

Over a month later, on a Saturday, Howard is running on the street near his building, and sees them. Rosa and the children. From behind. He runs harder to catch up. Reina is walking a step away, but Rico hangs close to his mother. Reaches up to hold her hand. Howard studies his back, where his T-shirt rides up. Comes closer, to see for sure.

He almost grabs her, stops her. To ask, *Who did that to Rico?* But it's a pointless question. She won't tell him, and he already knows. Breathe deeply, he tells himself. Slowly and deeply. But he feels deadly calm, and that is a bad sign. It's here. The moment. He's been dreading it so long, it's almost a relief.

He turns for home.

Howard pulls all his energy together. Trains it on the door of apartment 20K. Kicks. Waits. No sound from inside. Again. A splintering of wood. Again. He feels better. He throws his shoulder to the door, wood cracks and flies. Again. The door breaks free of its hinges. Falls.

Howard sits in the corner of the empty apartment. He knows from his watch that twenty minutes passes, but it doesn't seem that long until the man stands over his ruined door.

"You," he says. Strides across the room. "Get out."

The man moves to eject him, but he has underestimated Howard's strength. Howard pins him to the wall by the collar. His face close. The man is quiet in defeat.

"You got lucky," Howard says, "because you didn't run from me. I can't stand a man who won't hold still for his own consequences." Richard Bolt ran, he doesn't say. The man seems to have trouble breathing. Howard could help, but doesn't. "If you ever lay a hand on that kid again—"

"My kid. *My* kid. How dare you come into my home and tell me what I can do to my kid? How do you know I won't come back and kill you for that?"

"I don't."

"You assume I would not succeed?"

"I never make assumptions."

"To keep Rico from getting strapped you would die?"

"Twice."

Howard is uncomfortable with the changes in the man's face. It's a process he can't follow.

When the police announce their presence, Howard turns to see their guns drawn. He thought of the police, briefly, as he kicked the door down. It didn't matter.

The super stands in the open doorway with them. An officer tells them both to hold still. Asks the super to identify the intruder. The super points to Howard as if he always knew he would someday. As if it satisfies him.

"Okay, turn around and put your hands on the wall."

The man says, "That won't be necessary."

Everyone stares at him. The officers. The super. Howard.

"Sir, the man broke down your door."

"No. He didn't. I think somebody else tried to break in."

"He was assaulting you."

"That was just a misunderstanding."

Guns reholstered. "You sure?"

"Look, I don't need you here. Just go now, okay?"

The officers shake their heads. Shrug their shoulders at the neighbors gathered in the hall. "You can all go back to your own apartments now. Show's over."

The man declines to look at Howard, who goes home.

A little past midnight Rosa comes knocking on the door. Reina blinks beside her. Clings to her nightgown. Rico hangs limp on her shoulder, snoring lightly.

It takes Howard a moment to grasp that they are all right.

"Can I come in?"

Howard puts the children in his bed. He sits by the window with Rosa. He puts his arms around her shoulders. She is shaking. He has never wanted to kiss her more, but he knows this is not the time.

"Howard, I've never seen him like this. He's sitting in the corner. Just staring. He told us we should go. He said we'd all be better without him."

"He's right."

"I'm scared, though. I've never seen him like this. It's like he's dead inside. What happened, Howard? What did you say to him?"

He tells her as much as he can about the incident, but he can't answer her question. He doesn't know what happened to the man. Only what was said.

Howard braces a chair under the door. They lie on the floor together, he puts an arm over her to make her feel safe. He thinks she will never sleep but in time she does.

Howard wakes to the sound of sirens. Looks out the window, but he can see nothing.

Cautiously, he steps out into the hall. Looks through the open doorway into 20K. Looks in the bedroom. No one home.

Stepping out into the hall again, he sees it. Open. The door to the roof. A nightmare that repeats itself, but he has to see. He climbs the stairs. The air is frigid, sudden. The reflected glow of revolving red lights in the street. He walks to the edge. Looks down. Police cars. Ambulance. Onlookers. Lights trained on a body-sized lump, covered.

A police helicopter roars overhead. He can feel its wind, it ruffles through his grown-out hair. It shines a spotlight on the crowd in the street. Then it sweeps up to the roof. Howard looks up, it looks back at him. He blinks into the light.

When she comes to visit, Howard is taken from his holding cell, led into a small windowless room. She is waiting at a wood table. The guard stands with his back to the door.

They have ten minutes.

"I can't believe they think you killed him. They set your bail so high. I thought maybe I could post a bond somehow. But it's so high."

He puts his hand over hers. So small, it seems.

"I never expected you to. Where are the children?"

"With my mother. Howard—I can't believe I'm going to ask you this. Forgive me."

"I didn't kill him."

"I knew that. I knew you didn't. You couldn't."

"No. I could. But I didn't."

"Then it's okay, right? I mean, if you're innocent, your trial will come out okay. Right?"

Howard laughs. He realizes he doesn't laugh nearly enough. And it's not bitter. He has expected this, all of it, but it turned out better than he had hoped. He didn't kill again.

That takes a toll. "It's a nice theory. But, the thing is, there are some ugly coincidences that will work against me."

"So? Breaking a man's door down does not make you a killer."

"I wish that was the worst of it, Rosa. But we only have ten minutes. Later. I'll tell you more about me later."

"We could get you a good lawyer."

"We could?"

"Oh. Yeah. Money again."

"Always. Always money."

"I'll take care of you, Howard. I told you I'd take care of you, and I will. We take care of each other. Don't we, Howard?"

He smiles at the warm feeling inside. Chicken soup. Homemade. He knows she can't help but it doesn't matter. She holds his hand until the time is up.

She visits him every Sunday, awaiting trial. Even after he tells her about Richard Bolt.

Ralph, another inmate Howard knows, thinks Rosa is beautiful. But he says so in a respectful way.

"And your kids. Man. How does a guy like you make such pretty kids? No offense." He punches Howard lightly on the shoulder with this last sentence.

Howard takes no offense because he knows none is intended. He says, "The children look like their mother."

"Yeah, that's a break. Anyway, you're a lucky son of a bitch."

"Yes," Howard says. "I really am. I have been blessed."

He returns to his cell, top bunk. Smiles at the ceiling.

TORCH

1 RENATA

The candles my mother gave me were almost gone. She gave me a ton, I thought they would last forever. She'd say, "Only burn candles, Bernice." I could almost hear her say it, still, but it wasn't real. I mostly know what's real and what is not.

She called me Bernice because, well, that is my name, actually. Since she died I use Renata because I really hate Bernice, and I don't just mean the name, although that too.

I lit the third to last one, because I was happy but overexcited about Philip, and I held my hand over the flame until a blister happened. Only a little one, not like when my mother first sent me to see Dr. Melman. Still, I could hear what she would say. I told her *all my progress can't be made at once*, because Dr. Melman says that. This conversation was not real. My mother was not saying anything and neither was I. I mostly know what's real and what is not.

I sat out on the fire escape in the dark, and listened to sirens go by, watched their flashing lights and thought they might be my fear, but with a shape and a sound. I would like my fear better if I could hear it coming.

The blister on my palm was broken and kind of runny so I wiped it off on my skirt and went to bed.

I dreamed about the fish that fly in the air, only this time they did fine. Lately the fish tended to die when they swam above water. Dr. Melman said that was a good sign. Something about reality, which he understands better than I do.

When I woke up it was hot. Real hot. I could feel the sting of the burn in my palm, and I loved it for being familiar. I love anything I've always known, and can always know again. I always have.

I didn't write down my dream because why should I? I wasn't going to tell it to Dr. Melman anyway.

I got ready in front of the mirror, the way my mother showed me. She said I'm not an assertive person, but I can fool people into thinking I am. Like I can wear my suit with the shoulder pads, and I can stand up straight and tall. And I can make my voice lower, and more direct.

I practiced a little, like I always do, saying, "I'm here to collect the rent." Low and direct. Mother said I have a wispy little voice, like a child, and that makes it easy for people to walk all over me. And she was right. She knew a lot. Like, for example, one day she said it was time for me to learn to collect the rents. And she taught me how to do it. And then two months later she died, just like that. No warning. Now, how did she know that?

She also said, though, that I would have to be careful with men, that I would bring out the pedophile in them, but I don't think I bring out much of anything in men, unless I really try.

I always wear my Nikes to collect the rents. That is my own special touch. It's hard to be assertive in orthopedic shoes. The Nikes make me walk funny, with a roll, but by the time my tenants answer the door I am holding still, and I don't walk away until they give me the rent and go back in again.

I thought, because it was such a special day, the day after Philip looked at me, that maybe I could walk normal in my Nike shoes. And, you know, I think I did better, but maybe normal is asking too much. Still, I got all the rents, except

Mrs. Furley, who just got laid off at work, and she gave me half, so you tell me there's no magic.

2 PHILIP

It was one AM when Tom and I left that awful party. She stood in the circle of light from the streetlamp as we came down the stairs. The perimeter of light seemed oddly distinct to me, like a spotlight on a stage. From time to time I still wonder why.

She looked like a doll, or a little girl, or maybe both. She was hugging herself, her eyes cast down to the pavement in a deliberate gesture.

I knew I had seen her before.

Just as I walked by she raised her eyes and looked at me for one painful moment, and there it was, that excruciating mix of pain and joy that fragmented her from the inside out, and it seemed to somehow draw off of me.

I was sure that last part was my imagination.

She looked down at the street again and started to rock, and I looked back over my shoulder twice and wondered how anything so skinless survives in a world like this.

Tom was watching me out of the corner of his eye, wondering, I suppose. I couldn't explain the whole thing, of course, and god knows I am not the kind of man who looks at women in a lingering way on the street, and he of all people should know it.

I said, "I'm trying to think where I've seen her before."

Tom said, "Well, for starters, she was at Rumors tonight, down at the end of the bar, watching us dance."

I turned one more time to glance over my shoulder, but the circle of street light was empty, and, in her absence, somehow less distinct. I decided that the whole thing was not as strange as I had made it seem.

Then I didn't see her for a few weeks, not consciously, until that night I got so drunk, which is not like me as a rule. But it's this thing with Tom. He'd just got done telling me I want more out of this than he does, and that I'm too damned serious. And as far as monogamy goes, I didn't even dare ask the question, so we could hardly get a good fight going. Every now and then it's a good fight or a good drunk, nothing else will do.

Last thing I remember was being cut off by a bartender I thought was my friend. Suddenly it was morning, with the light like a razor in my eyes, so I didn't open them, but I knew I was in a bed much softer than mine, with these thin fingers running through my chest hair.

Curiosity overcame me. My eyes flickered open, and it was my friend from the street light, my little ghost.

She said, "Good morning, Philip," in just the tiny thin voice I would have expected.

She was tracing a path, up and down from my solar plexus to just below my navel, and it felt good. Problem was, I just couldn't think, with all the questions running around in my head, of a polite way to ask any of them.

"I hope you'll forgive me," I said, "because I was a little drunk last night—"

"Renata."

"Yes. Of course." I hadn't even thought of that one yet. "I almost don't know how to ask this, Renata, but like I said, blame it on the alcohol. Did we make love last night?"

"Sort of." She had a way of smiling like she was in pain.

"It's not you."

"I understand," she said precisely, pausing at every syllable. Third grade diction.

"Where do I know you from, Renata? I mean, before last night."

"Oh, everywhere. I see you all over town. I've been carrying a torch for you."

I hadn't heard that expression for years.

I smiled, and propped up with my hands behind my head, and noticed a camera on her dresser, a Nikon with a huge, long close-up lens, and beside it was a framed picture of me. It was a jolt I felt right down to my stomach. Me, through a telephoto lens, walking down a Manhattan street.

3 RENATA

The phone was on my lap and I could feel the weight of it. It rang, and I jumped, and picked it up and said, "Hello, Philip. I just knew you would call."

It was a wrong number. A Spanish-speaking wrong number.

I hung up the phone and made a nice dent in the wall with it, and then I went into my bedroom and opened the box and there were only two candles left from my mother. I still had the apartment building she gave me, I would always have that, but I needed something to burn. I could buy more candles but no way would it be the same.

I lit the second to last one. And I got all three newspapers, and I dropped them into my big metal wastebasket. And I picked up the penultimate candle and took the whole mess out on the fire escape. Slowly, so the flame wouldn't go out. And I dropped the candle in with the papers. It was the best bad thing I'd done for a long time.

With my back up against the rail I watched it, and oh, what a sight. Black smoke in columns up to the black sky. And showers of sparks catching on the wind and drifting down to the street. Three floors down they flew, like fireflies, only better.

A man with a shaved head walked by underneath me. "Hey lady," he called up. "Whatcha doin', lady?"

That and a distant siren were the only sounds. The only real sounds. My mother, reminding me to only burn candles, that was not real. I mostly know what's real and what is not.

Just for a minute, when the flame died and there was nothing left to protect me, I almost cursed Philip for not calling. Almost. But I found a way to turn it back on myself.

When the fire died I felt cold. And very dark.

I thought I'd never get to sleep, but it snuck up on me, like everything else. When I woke up I was still upset from my dream, but you can't write down what you don't remember.

4 PHILIP

I told Tom about her. He laughed at me. That hurt. The least he could have done was act threatened, and if it had been a man maybe he would have been.

He said she sounded crazy, maybe dangerous.

Truth was she scared me a little, too, but when Tom said it I wanted to defend her. He always says I scare him by being too intense, so it's a bit of a double-edged sword.

I made up my mind to tell her the truth.

I thought of every time I'd wanted to scream at Tom to just tell me the truth. Even if I'd hate it, have the guts to say it because nothing is worse than not knowing, nothing.

I'd thrown away her phone number, so I had to go by.

I knocked on the door, and she opened it, and almost jumped into my arms. She said, "Philip, I just knew you would come."

I felt about an inch high, but I told her that it wasn't going to be like she wanted. I said we didn't have to go back to being strangers again, we could always be friends.

Her face twisted into this pinched expression, and she started to pound on my chest, really giving it all she had, and the awful part was, it didn't even hurt. It reminded me of my little brother when he used to try to beat me up, and I'd hold him off with one hand and do my homework at the same time.

So she fluttered at me like a little bird on a plate glass window, and said, "That was what Ronnie said." I didn't know who Ronnie was, but I gathered that he had just wanted to be friends.

I took her by both wrists and sat her down on the couch and said I was sorry. I would always be sorry. But I had to go.

I knew then why it's so hard to watch someone go through that, why it's easier to run, and just for a moment I hated to be me, and I almost felt like I was her. Because I would rather be her than every asshole who ever dumped me, and those seemed to be my options.

Just as I was leaving, I looked back. She was wearing a long dress and big, strange shoes, with one sole maybe two inches thicker than the other. She saw me looking, and pulled her skirt down over her shoes, like they were the biggest secret she had. Even I couldn't know, and she loves me. I know, because she told me so.

I left her deflated and sobbing on the couch, wondering if that's how Tom sees me when I'm in the middle of one of my emotional firestorms.

I tried going back a few days later. Just to see if she was okay, and to tell her we could still be friends if that idea sounded better later on.

But she wasn't there. Nobody was.

The building was standing, but just a shell, all burned out and gutted, with window frames like cracked briquettes, and a line of police tape all the way around.

I made phone calls. All I could learn was that nobody had been killed. The landlady had evacuated all the tenants. But that was it.

I called all the hospitals, including Bellevue, and got them to scan their computers for someone with the first name Renata. This took some fancy talking, believe me.

Nothing.

It was a couple of months before I stopped looking over my shoulder for her. After awhile it becomes painfully clear that there's nothing you can do, so you do nothing.

Once, when I passed under a streetlamp, I wondered if any of the men in my life still look over their shoulder for me, and if I'm a ghost in anybody else's circle of distinct light, holding myself and rocking.

And I wondered: if I'd never met her, would I ever have wondered?

*T*he knock startled Jean out of sleep. She flung an arm out behind her, praying to strike Graham, but his side of the big bed lay empty. So she knew who waited at the door and why. But she was still too groggy to feel anything about it, which was good. In fact, it was her life's goal but it never worked well enough. Always there were loopholes and loose spots.

She pulled a robe on over nothing, made her way through the dark living room, and opened the door.

"David. I had a feeling it would be you."

"You know, if you can't find a way to put a stop to this, I'm going to have to."

It was the strongest statement she'd ever heard from him, and it pleased her. David was a soft boy, easily pushed, regularly bullied. And god knows she hoped somebody would put a stop to it. So she wouldn't have to.

He stood on her welcome mat in checkered pajamas under a red robe, brushing unruly masses of thick hair off his face, which he always did, even by day. A handsome boy, but he'd be the last to get a date, he might have a hard time getting girlfriends. Handsome needs something to back it up, make it a full set. Confidence, for example, or carriage.

He seemed impatient to bursting with the silence, the lack of resolution. "I can't sleep with this going on. I mean, doesn't she think I have ears? I'm not that heavy a sleeper. It's like she thinks I'm not even there. I'm in the next room, for god's sake."

"Would you like to come in?"

"You act like this doesn't bother you."

"The operative word being 'act'."

She took a step back from the doorway, a quiet invitation. He shifted his eyes down to the mat, then stepped in. He sat on the edge of her couch, his brow knit into furrows in the dim light. Only a little more so than usual. His face had succumbed to a constant worried scowl. Sixteen years old and already a victim of permanent knit lines.

"I'm going to have a drink," she said, then stopped herself. The obvious ending being *Would you like one?* He didn't carry himself like a boy, hadn't come to discuss boyish things, she had to remind herself. "Can I get you a Coke or something?"

He shook his head not so much to refuse the drink, she thought, but in wonderment and disgust, which she decided was warranted. He could not succeed in making her address this. She felt herself insist that the world spin along without anyone openly acknowledging this disaster.

"What happens if he walks in right now and sees me here?"

A good question. She poured herself a glass of brandy while she considered it. "I don't know." But she knew she was doing nothing to avoid it, perhaps another attempt to bring things to a head without direct, motivated action.

She sat on the couch beside him, watched him stare at his knees. "Where's your father, David?"

"Chicago. On business."

"When does he come home?"

"Tomorrow."

"Good. Maybe we'll all get some sleep tomorrow." She saw it in his face, the way that sounded. "I know. I need to confront Graham with this. You don't know him, though. If he even smells confrontation, he's gone."

He lifted his gaze from his knees to Jean's eyes. It made her uncomfortable when this soft, shy, nervous boy bested her strength. "I think gone is a good thing for Graham to be."

The lock turned quietly, and Graham stepped into the dark living room, his silhouette so huge against theirs, always the bigger shadow. "Jean? What are you doing up? Who's that with you?" His voice achingly familiar; that made it hard not to feel. Maybe two more drinks would be needed now.

David bristled like an animal over territory. She could read it through the air between them.

"Oh, it's David, honey. From across the street. He just thought he heard a prowler is all."

David's forehead knit more tightly. He remained silent.

"Oh. You know," Graham said, his voice faster and lighter, "I thought I heard something, too. That's why I was out. I think everything's okay, though."

"Yeah," David said quietly, for only Jean to hear. "Everything's just great."

He brushed past Graham and out the door. She wanted to stop him. Wanted to say, I'll talk to him. But she couldn't. Because she might not talk to him, at least not tonight. She might not be strong enough tonight. She might have been a minute ago, in his absence, but now in his big shadow she might not.

"What the hell was he doing here?"

"I told you."

"I don't like that kid. He's strange."

"I'm going back to bed." But morning came before she could get back to sleep.

First period found David sitting in the back of her creative writing class, early, before any other students arrived. Where he did not belong, because he was not her student. In an oversized, hooded, checked shirt, his hair no less unruly than it had been at two AM. She walked down the aisle to him, feeling disconnected, like a walk down the aisle at a wedding or down death row. Something of greater consequence than this.

Before she could open her mouth to speak, he handed her a transfer slip. "I'm in your class now."

"Why did you decide to transfer?"

"Because Mr. Rothenberg sucks. He only likes creative writing that isn't creative. He won't even let us use contractions. You should see how the stuff comes out sounding."

"Well, I hope you like it better here. I gave an assignment on Monday. A fable, no more than three pages. Did Mr. Rothenberg teach you about fables?"

"No, but I know what they are."

"It's due Friday. I'll give you an extension, under the circumstances."

"Friday's long enough."

"Okay, well, if you change your mind."

"You didn't talk to him, did you?"

A trio of students hit the room with even more noise and commotion than usual. Jean looked up to see two more boys follow, sift around for seats. Everybody liked to sit in the back, so the chance to talk privately was over.

A relief.

She found it hard to address the class in David's presence. He knew too much. Maybe he would stand at any moment and declare her a phony. Barely a card-carrying adult at all. But he sat quietly, never spoke or raised his hand. Still, his eyes.

He turned in his story on Friday, on time. She glanced at the title, "Paper Boy." And felt encouraged. Maybe it would be fiction. She shifted it to the bottom of the pile.

Once upon a time there was a boy. He wanted to get a job so his father would love him and be proud of him. So he got a job delivering the evening paper, but his father didn't notice, because his father was never home. But the boy did his job well anyway, just in case.

The boy's mother didn't notice he had a job, because she didn't know he was there to begin with. She thought he was a paper cutout of a son, just the one she always wanted. She didn't know he had a life outside of that.

Nobody ever called his house to say the paper hadn't come, or ended up on the roof or in the birdbath, because he always did his job right. He thought his customers would like him for that, but because he never let them down or made them angry they didn't notice he was there at all.

He'd deliver papers all afternoon and fall into bed tired, but he never slept well, because the man across the street came into his mother's bedroom while his father wasn't home. Which was always. So he got another job delivering the morning paper, to help him forget that he was tired in the morning, and why.

When the boy finally got to sleep he would dream he was made of paper, hardly there at all. Because if he was there, somebody would notice. If he was there, his mother would act like he could hear or would mind.

Then one morning he woke up and it wasn't a dream anymore.

He tried to do his job, but the wind kept blowing him off his bike. He had to hold onto mailboxes and streetlights to throw his papers. People looked right through him but he was used to that.

When the boy came to dinner his mother didn't notice the change. She smiled the way she always did.

That night, when he couldn't sleep, he opened the window and leaned out. He liked the sound of the wind in his ears, drowning out the sounds in the bedroom next door. But the wind picked him up and tried to pull him away. He held on to the window frame. The wind made him flap in the tree outside his room until he couldn't hold on anymore.

Then the wind took him away, and he didn't mind. In fact, he wondered why he had held so tight for so long.

The end.

Jean heard his voice behind her as she crossed the parking lot after the final bell. "You don't drive to work."

"Not usually. It's only a mile."

"Eight-tenths. Can I walk with you?"

"Sure. All right."

She remained careful not to look at him. Peripherally she could see him brush the hair off his forehead.

"I just wanted to make sure you didn't give me an A 'cause you thought you had to. I didn't come into your class to blackmail you for grades."

"I know that, David. I gave you the grade you deserved."

"So you really liked the story?"

"Yes. I really liked it."

"What did you like about it?"

She stopped walking and faced him. She looked at him, which seemed to make him uncomfortable. He hunched his shoulders and jammed his hands deep into his pockets, glancing around as if seeking asylum.

"Its honesty. It was emotionally honest."

"It's okay that it wasn't really fiction?"

"Nothing is really fiction."

"It didn't bother you?"

"Of course it did."

"I'm sorry."

"You're the only one involved in this who doesn't owe any-body an apology."

They walked in silence most of the way.

"Your mother is really beautiful." She waited until they reached their street to say it, then wished she hadn't said it at all. He didn't answer, and she couldn't watch his reaction.

Graham was home early from work, watering the lawn. He moved closer to the house when he saw David; David peeled away for home when he saw Graham, like the wrong end of two magnets. When she walked up the path, purposely avoid-ing eye contact, Graham moved to the backyard. More reverse magnetism.

She headed for the kitchen first, and got cookies and milk for herself. A regression. Four cookies later she felt his shadow at her back.

"Something about that kid I don't like."

"You mentioned that already."

"I think he's gay."

"Why would you say that? There's nothing effeminate about him."

"He's just so . . ."

"Sensitive?"

"I don't know. Something off about him."

"He's not macho, but that doesn't make him gay. Besides, what if he is? Why should you care?"

"I wish he wouldn't hang around you so much. I think he's in love with you."

"Make up your mind, Graham. Is he in love with me or is he gay?" At least pick an excuse to hate him and stick to it.

He never moved around her as they spoke, she never saw him. And it felt strangely natural. Graham wasn't somebody she saw, not really. Not anymore. Just a big shadow at her back.

"What were you two talking about?"

"He's in my class now. We were discussing a story he wrote."

"What was it about?"

"A boy who delivers papers."

"Oh."

Then no shadow at her back, but she wasn't sure where Graham had gone because she never saw him go.

Jean woke alone in bed. Why did she never hear him leave? And how dare he be so damn sure she wouldn't? And how awful that he was always right. Still, the carelessness of his MO struck her as an undisguised insult. She got up and poured a drink to help her consider whether he might have intended that.

She pulled back the living room curtain and watched the house across the street. What she expected the house to do was not clear, but it didn't do it, whatever it was. No lights, no movement, no answers.

Drawing her robe tightly around her, more for sustenance than warmth, she stepped out the front door. Crossed the street. Dreamlike. Too much so. In this dream state she decided she couldn't start a conversation about it over dinner. Or in bed at night. It was impossible to go from nothing to all this in a matter of seconds. But if she pounded on the door. Walked right in on it. He'd be the one to have to explain himself. He'd have to start talking.

She stood on the front porch feeling dizzy, and cold. Part of her wanted to go back inside where it was warm. A part with a loud speaking voice. Screw the long run. We're cold *now*. Let's get in out of this. She steadied herself on the door frame.

The door swung inward, and David burst out, almost slamming into her. He jumped back with a tiny scream.

They both held still, waiting for noise or movement upstairs, but nothing changed. Nothing ever changed.

They walked down the steps together, leaving the door open.

"I was just coming over to talk to you," he said.

"I know I've got to do something. I almost did. Just now."

"Don't let me stop you." He motioned back to the house.

"I think the moment passed."

He nodded, both disappointed and understanding. Or maybe she read too much in. They walked slowly toward the street.

"Not to tell you what to do. I was just coming over to talk to you. I wanted to talk to somebody."

"You want to go for a drive?"

"Yeah. Okay."

They drove in silence toward the river. David watched intently out the window, as if this was a valid pastime requiring full concentration, displacing conversation by need. Jean parked the car on Riverside Drive, where they could watch the steady pull of water in the moonlight.

He spoke first. "Did you know you're my best friend?"

"Well, thank you, David. But we don't know each other that well."

"I know."

"Time will come when you'll have lots of friends. And a girlfriend."

"What planet will I be on then?"

"It helps if you believe it."

"How can I believe something if I've never seen it?"

A good question, one Jean couldn't answer. But the conversation felt too evasive, anyway. If she couldn't talk to Graham she could at least be direct with this transparent boy. He knew most of her secrets anyway. "Do you have any idea how much it hurts me to have you see me like this?"

He turned to look openly at her. A rare occasion. "You look good."

"That's not what I mean."

"Oh. That."

"I'm a full-grown woman. There is no doubt that I deserve better than this. All I have to do is open my mouth and demand it. Well, it's not quite that simple. I have to be prepared to lose him."

"I don't see why that would be a bad thing."

A long sigh. The water so beautiful in the moonlight. So much nicer than anything else. Everything else. It made her wish she were floating in the moonlight, with or without a boat.

"I guess I don't either, in my head. But in here." She pointed to her gut, that hotspot of anxiety. The place she'd worked so hard to ignore. So hard. She was so tired. Maybe she wouldn't be able to do it much longer.

"You could find somebody better."

"What planet would I be on then?"

David smiled a little, and it made her smile just to see it. She wondered if he ever had before. "It helps if you believe it." An awkward moment, even compared to the others. "It's not like you were married to him."

"It's not that different from it, either."

They sat in silence for ten seconds, an hour. She wasn't sure. The water seemed to want to pull her in.

"Okay," she said. "I guess I've finally had enough. I'll put a stop to it one way or another."

"I'm really glad to hear you say that. Because I was about to solve the problem myself, and nobody would have liked my solution."

Jean drove them both home without asking what that meant.

Graham was home. In bed. She crawled in beside him, ready. She knew she was ready by her state of numbness. She could break into a million pieces on contact and never feel the pain.

"Hi, baby," he said. "Where'd you go?"

"Couldn't sleep. I just went out for a drive." *Baby?* Where had this tone come from, which sounded almost like affection?

"Where did *you* go, Graham?" Amazing. She'd said it. Through steel lips, hitting her ears hollow, like the voice of someone else entirely. But she hadn't promised to do this gracefully.

He rolled closer. Put his arms around her. His bigness changed in tone, back to what it had been originally. A comfortable blanket. "Do you know I love you, Jean?"

No. I don't. "I think so."

"No more midnight drives for either one of us. Okay?"

This might be the closest they'd ever come to talking something out. "I'll stay home if you will."

"Deal."

Nothing should ever be so easy. Or, at least, nothing ever had been before.

She couldn't remember exactly when they'd last made love. Before this. Too long, though.

She saw David on Main Street on a Sunday, hitchhiking. He had obviously seen her, and she could not pretend she wasn't going his way.

He settled quietly into the passenger seat, the tension a palpable commodity until he spoke. "We haven't talked for months. Not the way we used to."

"Really? It didn't seem that long."

"I feel like you've been avoiding me at school."

"Not on purpose."

"How do you avoid somebody by accident?"

She was so used to circumvention, so unused to being called on it. "Not consciously, is what I mean."

"I miss those long talks we used to have. I'm kind of sorry things turned out the way they did."

"How can you say that, David?" She heard a tone creep into her voice, a warning. More irritation than she felt. To back him down, perhaps. If so, unsuccessful.

"Because now you're never going to leave him."

Jean's face felt hot. Maybe looked it, too. Her secret fear, that maybe she was not as opaque as she liked to believe. "That's not necessarily true. Besides, when did this get to be about me? I thought this was about your mother."

"Both. So you *are* going to leave him?"

"I might. I think about it every day. It's like he's on this probation with me. Even though he doesn't know it. He'll have to give me a reason to stay. Or not. Soon."

A shift of his head toward the window. Whatever he was about to say, it made him look away. "He still did it. Even if he isn't doing it now. If you stay, then you just let him treat you that way. I would never treat you that way. I mean, I would never treat anybody that way. That's what I mean."

"Okay, David," she said. "Now I know what you mean."

She turned down their street, into her driveway, and he walked home, stopping once to look back. She knew because she looked back over her shoulder at the same time.

Graham had a bad habit of reading the evening paper in bed. Always an irritation, it had become a larger issue tonight. Big enough to factor into permanent decisions.

He threw section after section onto the floor as he finished, something else she didn't like. She watched, wishing he would talk to her. Wondering why he couldn't feel her stare. He could use a haircut, she noticed. A little shaggy. She reached out without thinking to brush hair off his forehead.

He grunted. "I'll be done in a minute."

She rolled away. Twenty minutes later he threw the last section on the floor, and turned off the light. He did not say goodnight. He should have said goodnight. She had already decided it was over if he didn't. Such a small price to keep her, and he couldn't seem to meet it.

She fell asleep willing herself not to soften overnight.

In the night she woke up as Graham got out of bed. Just going to the bathroom, she thought, but she heard him dress. When had she become such a light sleeper? A funny sort of progress. She lay awake with her eyes closed after he left. Thinking nothing. Enjoying that hollow, numb place where her thoughts used to be. A freshly erased blackboard.

Then she got up and walked to the window. Watched him cross the street. Thinking maybe it didn't matter anyway because she was already gone, and this would only make it impossible to go any way but forward.

Just as she started back to bed she heard a noise like a car backfire, but it didn't seem important. Nothing did.

Amazingly, she slept.

Then it was morning, with Graham still not home. She didn't try to get up, even though she knew she'd be late to school. Nothing wanted to move.

Until a startling, official knock. It said bad news, like a telegram in the middle of the night. Before she answered the door she knew.

She rode down to the station with the two policemen, filed a report which said almost nothing. After all, that's what she'd seen. Nothing.

Did the boy know the victim? the detective asked. Barely. Just to say hello. Did she know why Graham had entered the house? No. Did she have any additional information that might pertain? Anything at all? No. Things just happen.

While she sat at the detective's desk, she saw David ushered past, hair falling into his eyes, his face misshapen and red from crying. He wouldn't look at her.

Crying, maybe that's what everybody expected from her. Several people had already told her they were sorry. Maybe it was only the shock that kept her from understanding why they should be.

The detective said a uniformed officer would drive her home.

"What's going to happen to the boy?"

"Well, we're still questioning him, but I'm sure it'll be ruled an accidental shooting."

"Where did he get the gun?"

"His father keeps it in the house. And the father was away. You know how boys are. Probably felt like he needed to be the man of the house. Take care of his mother."

"Right. I understand. He's been edgy about prowlers."

"He should be home by the end of the day. He feels really bad about this."

"I know. I know him, he's in my class. He's a good boy."

"That's good, that you don't hold this against him. He feels bad enough."

"No. He's a good boy."

The uniform stood over her, empathetic bordering on patronizing. She rose and allowed herself to be driven home.

"You gonna be okay alone?" he asked on the drive.

"I think so." *It's just a fog. It will burn off, and then I'll know how I feel. It's a natural phase of grieving. I think.*

"Got someone to talk to?"

"Yes. I do." And she did. David would be home before the end of the day.

The cop walked her to the door. It felt good to close it, to make him gone.

She walked into the bedroom but couldn't remember why, so she walked out again. Graham's impression remained in the bed, the rumpling of sheets to accommodate him.

She sat at the window, looking out across the street, watching the line of police tape sway in the wind, and thinking, I never have to try to make that awful man love me again. A light feeling. The fog had burned away, leaving the unexpected.

Relief.

She sat on the lawn of his house until the police car dropped him home. Even though it was cold.

His face registered panic, but she smiled. And waved him over. He sat beside her in the damp grass, his face still puffy from tears.

"You didn't tell them. You could have screwed me up good. Why didn't you?"

"I don't know how to explain it. It's like I finally made a real decision. And that was it. Where's your mother?"

"I think she's upstairs. But she's—you know. Tranquilized."

"Oh." A strange thought. That beautiful stranger upstairs lost the same lover I lost. Only she's taking it harder.

They sat quietly for awhile, and she put her arm around his shoulder.

"When I was a kid," he said, "my cat ate my parakeet. It was a really hard thing. I wanted to hate her, but she was my cat. My little Emily. I'd had her almost all my life."

"I don't hate you."

"I know. I can tell. I don't know why not, but I'm really glad."

"You don't have to go to court or anything?"

"No. They ruled it accidental."

"That's good." Jean could hear herself talk like a sleepwalker, but it was a kind of peace, and any kind would do. "I think I'll try to get a good night's sleep."

She stood up. Tired. Sleep would feel good. She wouldn't have to wake up and check his side of the bed. Ever. A brutal kind of freedom, but any kind would do. "Just so I know for sure, David. Just between you and me. Did you really think Graham was a robber? Or did you know who it was?"

"Graham *was* a robber." Standing a bit outside herself, Jean watched herself nod slightly. "I had to do something. Sometimes you can't just wait for things to change. You have to do something."

"I know. I learned that from you."

She reached down and brushed the hair off his forehead before heading home to sleep.

MRS. MULVANEY, THE GRASSHOPPER GOD

I was having a soda one afternoon with Roger Eaton when The Idea arrived. I was minding my business at the time and really not attempting to be cosmic at all. It was the hottest part of a New Jersey July, and the red and white patio awning failed to cover a small strip of my back, which perspired into the cotton sundress Roger particularly liked. Here and there ants scurried across the table, blind to the fact that humans hate it when they do. Roger would press a finger onto each one to snuff it and then flick it onto the concrete of Amelia's Sweet Shoppe patio.

As he snuffed and flicked, he discussed the war in Europe, a subject close to his heart, as he had three grandsons overseas. Two, I should say. One had just been killed in France.

"Doesn't god seem awfully random to you, Emily? Do you ever wonder why my grandson must be killed while someone else's gets to come home? Do you think there is rhyme and reason to it, Emily, a plan, or do you think god is less than properly concerned about who he kills, and why? No, don't answer that—these are only the ramblings of a bitter old man. We all want to know why god does what he does, but who can say?"

"Yes, I suppose that's why we need god, he understands so much that we muddle with."

I sipped my soda and watched Roger snuff ants, and that was when The Idea arrived, because there was sweet, if not so awfully sharp, Roger, by no means a violent man, attending to acts of random killing. Oh, it might not seem like much to you, but if your children were ants, and you were one too, then see how you'd sit up and take notice.

If I'd asked Roger about this killing spree, asked him the question we so long to ask god, *why?*, I could tell you just what he would say. With a minimum of guilt, he would say he murdered them because they were on the table. Roger, who did like to go on, might have added some information about the transmission of disease or what have you, but the real gem of wisdom is contained in the original statement. They were on the table. They were in his way.

The Idea is that maybe god snuffed Roger's grandson and flicked him onto the patio because he was trying to enjoy a soda, and the kid didn't know enough to keep off the table.

I shared no details of The Idea with Roger, because I am sane enough to know that I have earned somewhat of a reputation as an eccentric, one I don't mind too terribly, but still, why fan the flames? In addition, I suddenly had nothing left to say to Roger the Ant Killer, and, in fact, the Roger era of my life was very much over.

Besides, The Idea really took shape the following day, as I prepared for my every Sunday afternoon task, cutting the grass. Oh, and it is a production. Everybody seems to have an opinion about the cutting of my grass, and everybody seems to be of the opinion that their opinion should be heard.

My grown son Emmett feels I should at least use a mower with a motor, if I was going to try to cut my own lawn at my age; hard not to hear the veiled insult there. He had one so equipped, and gave it to me for Christmas, and there in the corner of the garage it sits. Emmett accuses me of being old-fashioned, and not accepting modern ideas, but it's not so complicated as all that. It's more that the immense power of the thing impresses me as an out-of-control sort of power, dangerous and beyond me, and besides, try as I might, I can't seem to pull that string hard enough to kick the thing into life.

My next door neighbor, Arnold Felker, doesn't care who cuts my lawn, or with what, but firmly believes it should be cut a half-inch shorter, so as not to look so ratty and unkempt next to his own.

Most everyone agrees on one point, however, that one should begin cutting at a corner and proceed in straight lines. I have no argument with how they cut their lawns, and wish to be left in peace about my own. It's easier to push the darned mower if you let it swoop around in whatever patterns it pleases to go, and more creative and fun besides, and as long as it all gets cut, who's to judge?

The neighbors ramble out onto their porches and shake their heads, and when I take my break partway through, for my lemonade, some stranger will invariably wander by, stare dizzily at the maze of patterns, and trot quickly away.

On the day in question I set the mower at the middle edge, and rushed toward the center of the lawn, curving my first stroke into a lovely crescent moon. This is when The Idea came back, much richer and more fraught with implications—so much so, in fact, that I took my lemonade break early.

Is god really so different from a woman cutting the grass, thinking she has a purpose far greater than the crickets, grasshoppers, ants, bees, who will die horrible deaths? Is the cosmetic appeal of the lawn really so important? To us, maybe, but nobody asks them. Imagine life from their level: the whirring, clacking blades, destroying families, uprooting homes, little insect body parts flying. What would be the human equivalent? A dreadful hurricane, perhaps? And when the every Sunday task is over, do they react as we do? Stand among the corpses and the rubble asking, "Why, god? Why?"

Suddenly I saw the world in layers, stratas of gods and subjects, priorities leading to the destruction of the small. Indeed, on the next level we are the small, and pity those who forget it.

Long into the evening I sat on my front porch, the ice all melted in my lemonade glass, imagining the colonies spared on my front lawn. The moon rose in a lovely crescent to match the one I'd carved into the world of my subjects, confirming that everything balances with everything.

If one is going to be a god, it is every bit within one's control to be a ruthless god, or a benevolent god.

Arnold Felker, my neighbor, was ever so polite, at first. He stood on my doorstep with his baseball cap in his hand, saying, "A gracious good morning to you, Mrs. Mulvaney. I can't help noticing that your grass hasn't been cut three weeks running, and I can certainly see what a big undertaking it is for you, though I must say you're in marvelous health for a woman in your golden years. Anyway, I'd be happy to do the job for you."

"Oh, no," I said. That's all. Just, oh no.

"I see. Well, who is going to cut it, then?"

"Oh, nobody's going to cut it."

"Ever?"

"Ever."

"I see. Did I mention there would be no charge? Just helping beautify the neighborhood."

"You're very kind, Mr. Felker"—only not below your strata—"but you just attend to your own kingdom and trust me to take care of mine."

And I closed the door, not hard, nor rudely, but quite enough to end the conversation.

The kingdom of Mulvaney was a beautiful jungle when Mr. Felker took the matter before the town council, complete with snapshots of not only my lawn, but his own as well. Photographic proof that not one blade of crabgrass was to be found anywhere on his beautiful green carpet, of which he was right to be proud.

The council unanimously concluded that it was my property and my jungle, and I could not be forced to comply with anyone else's lawn code.

After the meeting, the council informally concluded that Mr. Felker was normally a pretty reasonable man, and probably just under extra pressure, what with having two sons over in the Pacific and all. Probably when they marched safely home he'd come around again to the idea that this lawn thing was not the most important way to spend one's life energy.

And after Arnold Felker had spent three more weeks of life energy grumbling and growling about it to anyone who would listen, up to and including a reporter for WKBG radio, who bumped the story for a garage fire in the south section, he turned out on my lawn in the middle of a Tuesday night. It was a moonlit Tuesday night, with plenty of light to cut grass by.

I might never have noticed, save for the fact that I had been wakened by a touch of indigestion, and was standing in the kitchen fixing a bicarbonate of soda when Mr. Felker arrived. I crossed over to the kitchen window to investigate the choppy little hacking noises, and saw Mr. Felker attempt to push a lawnmower against the edge of my jungle, most un-successfully.

I shook my head and hurried off to the closet in search of the late Mr. Mulvaney's twenty-two, the one he used to control gophers in the backyard, years before he died, and before, in his absence, I came to understand about the stratas of life.

Mr. Felker left when the twenty-two was shown to him.

"You haven't seen the last of me," he said.

The next day Viola Thompson came by to drive me to the podiatrist downtown, who kept me waiting a full fifty minutes longer than usual—and the usual is bad enough. And sure enough, upon arriving home, we could not help but to notice that my beautiful jungle kingdom was gone, and the neighbors turned out on their lawns, or peeked out their windows, to see what my reaction would be.

They must have been disappointed, because all I would do was to say, "Why that hateful, spiteful man," in a quiet voice, and then Viola said, "Never you mind, dear, we'll just go inside and have a cup of tea."

Over tea, Viola asked why I wanted the grass long, anyway, and I tried to explain, as best I could with a difficult concept, about the grasshoppers and the stratas of life.

"That's interesting," Viola said, "and it reminds me of a newsreel I saw once, though I can't remember where, only that it was about a religious order in Africa—or was it India? Well, no matter. They devote their lives to not harming any living thing. They carry little brushes to brush the ground they walk, or the seat they sit on, and they only eat certain beans and fruits and such that can be picked without damaging the plant. I wish I could remember where I'd seen that, but I remember only that it preceded an old movie with Ramon Navarro—or was it Francis X. Bushman?—and maybe that's why I remember it, I remember everything better if it's associated in my mind with Francis X. Bushman. My, he was a piece of work."

Everything is a piece of work I thought, but did not say. Still, being a human woman and not yet dead, I did see Viola's point about Francis X. Bushman.

When Viola finally left, I walked to Mr. Felker's house and knocked. When he answered, I said, "I must assume, Mr. Felker, that you are the party who cut my grass. Am I correct?"

"You are," he said.

"Fine," I said. "That is all I cared to know."

After which I went home and called the police and had Arnold Felker arrested, and after some debate as to what the charges should be, charged with destruction of private property and trespassing. He paid a thirty-five dollar fine and promised to devote thirty hours to public service, and by the time he arrived home the neighborhood had heard Viola's version of why I did not want the grass cut. The neighbors were not slow to share this news with Mr. Felker, and, as I might have imagined, it served to anger him.

He pounded on my door and shouted at me and said, "You had me put in jail over a bunch of grasshoppers?" And he shouted this louder than necessary, and not in the voice of a sane man, but rather one who's been under too much pressure, what with this and that.

I opened the window to address his concerns just as he began to jump around on my lawn, shouting, "This is what I think of your grasshoppers, Mrs. Mulvaney, I am jumping up and down on your grasshoppers."

And he did.

"I will say a prayer for you tonight, Mr. Felker. I will pray that the god who watches your sons overseas is a kinder and more benevolent god than you are."

"You leave my sons out of this," he bellowed. "My sons are more important than your grasshoppers!"

"Well, to you, yes, I'm sure they are, Mr. Felker, but I'm wondering, would the grasshoppers agree? That your sons are more important than their sons, that is."

By this time, of course, the neighbors were all turned out, and they remained so long after the police had come and arrested Mr. Felker for trespassing and creating a disturbance. This time he did not come back for three days.

A few weeks had gone, and my grass was several inches high when Mr. Felker and his wife received the news that one of their sons had been shot down over the island of Tinian. Cars lined the streets as friends came to sit with and console them, and as Mr. Felker walked the last of them to their cars, he spotted me sitting on my porch, fanning myself, and the combination of my lawn and my presence seemed to overwhelm him.

"This has nothing to do with your grasshoppers," he shouted from his own driveway. "It has nothing to do with what kind of god I am. God and I have nothing to do with each other! There is no comparison between me and god!"

"Well said, Mr. Felker," I replied, continuing to fan.

Arnold Felker sold his house and moved to the south side, where he would not have to watch my grass grow.

And grow it did.

LEARNING TO TALK

*A*melia prided herself on knowing something of the workings of a combustion engine. There was more she did not know, but she minimized this. Still, there is a special sound to expensive damage, a clear, unmistakable engine noise. Valves rattled. Compression fell off in stages, with Tuba City miles behind and Second Mesa miles away.

For nearly a year she had dreamed of the Painted Desert, and now she wanted nothing more than never to have come.

Scenery ranged from nothingness to scatterings of shack dwellings. One lane in each direction, no other car in sight.

The Fiat tried to stall, but Amelia downshifted to first. It sputtered and trudged on. As she headed up a hill, the clattering turned to banging, the hood seeped blue smoke, the engine died. Amelia's knuckles whitened on the wheel. She prayed to reach the crest. No, not prayed. She hated people who did that. Unless they did it often, even when they weren't in trouble, in which case she simply failed to relate to them.

At three miles per hour the Fiat crested the hill. She squeezed her eyes shut, then looked again. Nothing. Too slow to register on the speedometer. Amelia threw open the door and pushed with her left foot. The road fell away. She drew a breath as she hit forty, then wondered what she had accomplished. Then the sign. LAST GAS BEFORE SECOND MESA. The ancient single gas pump blended with the private junkyards, the old-tire retaining walls. Only the sign called attention. Behind it, a shack smaller than her garage. A pay phone.

She stamped the brakes and skidded across the sandy dirt into Last Gas. It got attention from an old man sitting on a straw bale in the shade and an Indian pumping gas into his Ford pickup.

Her cowboy boots struck soft dirt, and her legs felt long as she stood. She forced the sense of it, pressed to reacquaint herself with herself. She would need that

"Engine runs quiet on that foreign jobber." The Indian.

"Yeah, when it runs. You fellows know a good mechanic?"

The old man wandered up, fumbled for the hood latch. Had he never heard of a hood pull in the driver's compartment?

"What seems to be the trouble?"

"Or maybe even someone with tools they'd let me borrow? Or rent? I could probably fix it if I had the tools."

The old man's eyes came up. "Howd'ya get under this hood?"

She sighed and released the hood from inside.

The Indian joined him, and they leaned in together.

"Start 'er up."

"Guys. If I could, we wouldn't be having this conversation."

The Indian pulled his head clear, replaced his wide-brimmed hat. "Lady. We're trying to help you. Just turn the key."

Amelia dropped hard into the driver's seat. Hit the ignition. Metal clattered and screamed. Blue smoke plumed.

"Holy cow, lady, shut 'er down."

"Whoo-ee."

"Shit," Amelia hissed under her breath.

"We better call Travis."

"Shoot, what does Travis know about a little foreign jobber?"

"Travis can fix anything."

"Look, guys." Amelia's boots stamped hard through the

dusty lot. "I'm not helpless. I know something about cars."

The old man broke into a grin which showed two missing teeth. "Then how come you didn't change the timing belt?"

The Indian pushed his hat back. "Then why drive a Fiat?"

"Hey. A Fiat is a good car."

"No, a Ford is a good car."

And the Indian jumped in his pickup and pulled away, sending a cloud of dust to settle on Amelia and the old man.

"I'll just use your phone. Call for a tow."

"Can if you want. But it's seventy miles to the nearest real station. Travis works pretty cheap. You might have to look after the baby while he works, but it'd save you a bundle."

Amelia walked away from him, toward the station. She crossed the old wood decking, listening to her boot heels sounding substantial and safe. She bought a bottle of Coke from an ancient, bubble-shaped red machine, uncapped it and took three cold, welcome swallows. How much money did she have left? Could she really bring herself to call Gordon and ask for help? She turned to find the old man staring.

"Well, don't just stand there," she said. "Call Travis."

Travis said nothing. Just held the baby out for her to take, a bundle of dark infant boy wrapped in a folded white sheet.

She took a step backwards. "You know, people just assume that because I'm a woman I must be maternal, but really I don't relate to babies. At all."

Travis took a step in, placed the bundle in her arms, and brushed past her to the Fiat. The child began to fuss. Amelia bounced him awkwardly, and glanced up at the old man.

"Friendly guy, that Travis."

The old man smiled and shuffled into the shade to sit.

Travis stood at the driver's door and pushed the Fiat around behind the station, where a sheet of corrugated plastic on poles formed a shady work area. Amelia followed, rocking the fussy baby. Babies smelled her discomfort, she was convinced.

"So, the thing is, Travis, I'm a little short on cash. I mean, I have some, but I'd like to save a little if I can, so maybe somebody else could watch the baby and I could help you. I do a lot of my own repairs. I could cut down on your time."

Travis pushed past her and reached in to pop the hood.

Amelia sat in the dirt against the rear wall of the station, watching Travis with a growing sense of unease.

He was practically a kid. Maybe twenty at best. A tall, lanky man with straight black hair combed along his head, half curving up at the base of his neck, half disappearing into his collar. He had the heavy brow and deep-set eyes of an Indian.

She bounced her knees slightly to keep the child amused. "So, Travis. You always talk this much? Some people don't like all that chatter. But I don't mind."

Travis straightened, sliced through her with his eyes, then walked to his truck for tools.

Amelia watched his back, then realized she preferred to be elsewhere when he returned. She bought a Coke and joined the old man indoors.

"Does Travis talk?"

"Only if something really needs saying."

The baby fussed again, and the old man showed her how to quiet him by running the cold Coke bottle against his cheeks.

"He's just hot, is all. Aren't ya, Edward?"

"You know this kid pretty well."

"Know him? This here's my great grandson."

"Where's his mother?"

"Died giving him birth."

"Oh. I'm sorry."

"Wasn't your fault."

"That's a point."

Gordon picked up on the fourth ring. A bad sign.

"Wakeman and Richards."

"Gordon."

"Amelia. Are you home already? I'll have to call you back."

"No, Gordon. I'm—not home. It's sort of an emergency." Oh, good. That's telling him. I'm nowhere, needing car parts that aren't even made in this country. Sort of an emergency.

"But I . . . Amelia, hold on."

A hot wind blew into Amelia's eyes as she waited. The operator broke in, wanting more money. She paid it out of a dwindling pocketful of change. If he kept her on hold much longer . . .

"Amelia. Where the hell are you? What's up?"

"I need a favor, Gordon. A big one." Like please don't give me a hard time about this. "I need parts for the Fiat. And I need them shipped on the fastest delivery. And other than that place in Glendale, I don't even know who imports them anymore."

Silence. Then: "I'll wire you money. Leave the damn car to rust and come home."

"Gordon. Please."

"Okay. But after this you'll get a new car. Right?"

"It's my fault, Gordon. I didn't replace the timing belt."

"Right?"

"You know I can't afford one."

"No. You *could*, Amelia."

She held the receiver in both hands, ready to hang up. But what then? This was the problem with needing anybody. For anything. She returned it to her ear.

"I'll pay you back for the parts, Gordon. Send them to Travis Newton, general delivery, Second Mesa, Arizona. I need two pistons, a full set of valves. A gasket set. And there was something else. Shit. What else did he say?" The operator broke in again. Amelia fed the phone her last six quarters. "Oh, yeah. Make sure they come with valve stem seals."

"Okay. Look, are you going to be all right?"

"Oh. Gordon. I also need a new timing belt."

"You also need a new car. But we'll talk when you get home."

Travis turned the old International Harvester up the road to his house and found his voice.

"People will talk," he said. "Will that concern you?"

"People? There are people around here?" Then she decided she'd said the wrong thing. Again. She held the little bundle of baby closer to her chest. Watched Travis in profile. The way she felt now, maybe she'd give them something to talk about.

"I'll take care of the baby while I'm here. It's the least I can do. I'll even wake up with him at night. I'll have to get a credit card advance when we go pick up the parts. But you'll get paid. No matter how much it comes to. If I have to, I'll get Gordon to wire more money."

Travis stopped the International, took the baby back into his arms. Amelia followed him into the house. Shack. No, house. Modest, but clean enough and proud enough to be called a house.

"But you don't want to do that."

"Do what? Oh, Gordon. No, I don't."

When Edward cried in the night, Amelia stumbled up and ran to him, but her reflexes were slow. Travis was already at his side. His back faced her as he lifted his son from the crib and carried him to the window. The desert moon washed them in light as Travis began his motion, a strange form of rocking which seemed to border on slow dancing.

As he rocked his own body in one direction, he rocked Edward in the other, his head bent low, for what purpose Amelia could not see. As he turned to replace the sleeping child in his crib, she realized he had been stroking his cheek against the top of Edward's fluffy head.

He saw her then, and smiled, as if to say *Good of you to come, but it's all handled.* Amelia had never before seen him smile. In fact, she suddenly believed she had never before seen him. Although she liked to study the dark hair on his arms as he worked, or look at his eyes and guess what he didn't say, that, she now realized, was a type of survey, not true vision.

He brushed past her to his own room, and Amelia felt vaguely insulted, though she had been prepared to squelch any advance. It now seemed foolish to have thought there might be one.

In the morning she tried her own cheek against Edward's black hair. It reminded her of the silkiness of her mother's old fox coat, and the way she would pretend to fall asleep against her mother on long car rides as a way to cuddle closer to that strangely comforting fur.

Edward smiled and grasped a lock of her hair. Amelia wondered with dread rather than impatience when the car would be fixed. She asked to come to the station to watch Travis work.

The baby slept in the shade by her side, and Travis lay on his back under the engine compartment. Now and then his hand would reach out for a tool, his arms black to the elbow.

"So, the old man said he's your grandfather."

A disembodied voice from the crippled engine. "No."

"No? That's what he told me."

"You misunderstood."

"Oh, wait. I get it. Your wife was his granddaughter. Oh. That must have been awfully hard on him, when she died. I mean, not that it wasn't hard on you. Oh, shit. I'm talking too much again. Why did I start talking about that? I'm sorry."

After a long silence, Travis grabbed the bumper and slid out. He sat up in the dirt and wiped his hands on a greasy shop rag. His eyes burned her with their directness.

"It's okay."

Amelia found herself with nothing to say for once.

"He'll sleep for awhile. Come on. You can help me."

Amelia inched under the jacked-up engine and removed the oil pan bolts from one side while Travis worked on the other. Bits of greasy dirt fell into her eyes, and now and then her bare arm brushed his accidentally. She said excuse me. He said nothing.

When the baby fell asleep for the night, Travis took up a book, as always. Amelia stared for a few minutes.

"You know, Travis . . ." His eyes did not come up. "I've been hanging around here for almost five days, and you haven't said ten sentences to me."

Travis set his book face down and open on the arm of his worn chair, but remained silent.

"See, in my line of work, we rely on words. Completely." She waited for him to ask what she did, then wondered when she would learn. "I'm a freelance journalist. We think the whole world revolves around words. Like they're the only key to communication. I used to think they were really worth something. But now I'm not so sure."

Silence.

"Nobody understands why this line of work is so important to me. Least of all Gordon. He thinks I should get a real job. But I thought there was something in all those words. Some help for me. You know? I used to think we were all looking for something. After something. But you're not. Are you?"

Travis rose to his feet. "I don't have what you're looking for," he said. He headed for his bedroom.

"Travis." He turned back. "Don't you like me at all?"

She listened to her own words hang in the air, the perfect fragility of a sudden, undisguised romantic question.

Travis breathed quietly. "You've come here three months after a big loss. Come three years after. I may like you better."

"But—" She found herself speaking to an empty room. She ran after him, stopped the door to his room as he swung it closed. "What is it with you, anyway? You don't show the first thing about how you feel. How can anyone even know you?"

"Do you see that I am grieving?"

"Well, of course. Anyone would see that."

"Then you know all there is to know about me for now."

His door closed, and she stepped back to allow it.

In the dark hours of morning, still awake, Amelia stole into the living room to read the book Travis had left open on his chair.

She saw him standing at the window, his back to her, and she watched the motion of his shoulders and decided he must be crying. No sooner did she conclude this than Edward woke up and began to wail, as though he and Travis were connected in some unearthly way, and she bolted to the baby, hoping Travis wouldn't see her when he turned around.

She rocked the baby at the window, and rubbed her cheek against his soft hair, and he reached his hands up to touch her face, just reached for her, just like that, and she knew that it was not Travis, but Edward, who held answers. If Travis could cry, surely he had learned it from the boy, this child who would simply reach out for love if that was his need.

Amelia told Edward that he was the only man in her life who understood all of what was going on here. That seemed to please him.

"Okay," Travis said. "That's it."

The Fiat ran smooth and quiet, idling by itself in the dusty lot. "How much?"

"A hundred fifty dollars."

"No. No way, Travis. That was almost six days work. A city mechanic would have charged five times that."

"A city mechanic wouldn't have taken six days."

"It's not enough."

"It's enough. It's my price. An independent woman like you shouldn't have to call Gordon."

"I guess this means I'll have to be going."

"You don't have to do anything. Edward likes you. Stay or go, as you choose."

Amelia lay awake until she realized that the silence in Travis's house had become a sad burden. Or at least, a sign of foreign territory. Not home.

She wrote him a note before leaving. It said, "Love is always now. Only now. There is no such animal as love three years down the road. But maybe I'll come back and visit the boy sometime. That is, if I'm still welcome."

For the first twenty or so miles, the road home seemed to point in the right direction.

But Edward would be learning to talk soon, and he might reveal some of his secrets. And Travis, he might be learning to talk soon, too.

ALICE NEEDS THIS

*S*he'll say she is sixteen, but she's probably fourteen, if that. She is overweight, and she will not wear a swimsuit at any time during her stay. If she goes for a swim in the lake she will wear shorts and a T-shirt, she is that ashamed. She'll say she burns easily, as if I can't see her shame. As if I don't know her.

She has a name that she hates. She has never had a serious boyfriend.

She sits on the dock, dangling her feet into the water.

"Hi," I say, loud and cheerful, as though I was a regular man, and one she might meet without fear. That is best for now. Later she will know I am to be feared, but she will love me anyway. She already does.

She has passed the point of no return, like that terrifying break of rapids on the Niagara River, the spot where I used to stare as a boy, for an hour, for two, until my father or my brother found me and dragged me home. Staring and wondering how it would feel to be in the grip of such an irresistible force, to have lost mastery over one's destination, over one's very life.

Another part of me already knew.

I administer the first test. "You're new around here, eh? What's your name?"

She is looking deep into me, trying to find it again. Good girl. She says her name is Alice.

"Alice. My, my. Alice. What a lovely name."

She wrinkles her nose. "I hate the name Alice," she says.

"Really? Do you really? I'm surprised."

I will tell her a few other lies at the outset, but we will get down to the truth and she will be ready to hear it.

"Do you like to fish, Alice?"

"Well, yes," she says, "only not with my father, and he's the only one who ever takes me, but he's so . . . oh, I don't know."

Yes you do, Alice, and so do I.

"Picky?" I say. "Always makes you feel like you're not doing things his way?"

"How did you know?" she says.

"I know," I say. "I understand. I had a father, too." I say, "Maybe tomorrow we'll go out on the lake and do some real fishing."

She says she'll ask her parents, but I know it's better if I ask. And besides, there is her mother, puttering about in front of the cabin, where no puttering is required, wondering who her daughter is talking to and why.

"Hello," I call to her mother. "Welcome to the lake. My name is Adam Thurman. I was just talking to your daughter about fishing. Maybe one of these days you'd let her come out on the boat with me."

Mrs. Cardboard has the high, insipid voice I expected. "Well, I'm sure that would be just fine, Mr. Thurman, if that's what Alice wants."

Believe me, lady, it's what Alice wants. In fact, it's what she needs. I have something Alice needs, and she will follow me to the ends of the earth for a taste.

And before you think me completely uncouth and revolting, I must say that I am not referring to sex. Alice doesn't need sex. She needs to be looked at as though she was there. She needs love she can feel. She needs to believe, if for only a moment, that she is alive.

She needs it enough that she'll accept the sex as part of the package. Happily.

By the way, my name is not exactly Adam Thurman. It's Wesley Adam Thurman. My real first name is Wesley.

But I want Alice to call me Adam. Because to her, that's what I am. Adam.

Alice catches two lovely lake trout, and tells me all about her parents, as if I didn't know. As if I didn't have parents of my own.

I tell her I know exactly how she feels, but I can tell she has heard that line before; or rather, when she heard it before, it was a line.

I say, "You feel as though you can't feel. As though you are living in an utter void of transmission, like the white noise of television when you wake up to find that you've fallen asleep. And your worst fear is that everything is being transmitted just fine, and you are left with a defective receiver, and it feels like watching everyone chatter and hearing only deafness."

She stares at me for a few seconds and swallows. She is well into her stage of modesty, as if to be seen is to be seen naked. No, more than naked: exposed in a more vulnerable way.

She says she didn't exactly know she felt that way, or she wouldn't have known to use those words, but I am right, of course. She says she has never met anybody like me.

I could have told her that yesterday, if her boat hadn't skimmed by so fast.

Now and then something will remind me that there is a god running things, if indeed *god* is the right word. I use the word, but advisedly, because I have come to hold the tenuous opinion that he is perhaps no healthier an individual than yours truly.

Before we bring our little boat ashore, I begin to feel the charge of a good electrical storm, a summer thundershower. The clouds drift in, feeling ominous, and the light begins to turn that strange color and weight, and if you take a deep breath you can feel it. You can feel the charge.

I don't know if it will arrive at sunset or in the dark of night but I know Alice and I will celebrate.

Together.

So I begin my initiation, with the help of this god whose motives I doubt.

By the time I have rowed us home, Alice will not only

understand why I love electrical storms, why they make me feel so alive, she will love them every bit as much as I do.

It's contagious, this need to feel alive.

She will go home wanting tonight's storm, anticipating it. Loving it as much as she loves me.

Long webs and nets of lightning crackle through the sky on the far side of the lake, and I can hear it. Not just the thunder, I can hear the lightning. It sounds electric.

And I can feel it, in that empty place in my gut.

And I can see Alice approach in the light of the flashes, stealing from her house, unseen except by me.

And I realize Alice will want to be kissed.

Sometimes I must be careful with these details that vary from my own experience.

She sits down beside me and we watch the lightning crackle, and hear it, and feel it, without saying a word. That is how close we already are.

But I do use words to explain that I am going to kiss her. I am going to kiss her because I care for her and feel so close to her, and because it seems the best possible way to celebrate the miracle of this storm. And I go on to explain that I would never hurt her by doing anything against her will but only to protect my own reputation in my own head, because Alice has no will to go against.

Already she is grabbing my shirt, wanting to be close.

So I lay her back on the ground and kiss her and she is absorbed into me, which is what she wanted from the start.

Alice needs this.

As I unbutton her blouse I tell her that I am the only one who understands her, and that I will protect her and give her the attention she so deserves, all of which she knows, but wants to hear just the same.

My jeans sail partway down the hill and hers remain hooked over one of her feet, and she lets out a little cry which might be pain, but still she clings to me. And I coo gently in her ear to soothe her, reminded in a powerful flash of Manny, and the way he used to kiss my tears away when it hurt.

He would say, "There is good pain and bad pain, Wesley.

There is pain that reminds you that someone loves you. That I love you."

I cherished that pain for two days or more at school, every time. And it was always the best two days, sitting on that hard wooden chair, shifting around to better feel the pain, to be reminded that Manny loved me.

So I say it, too. I say, "There is good pain and bad pain, Alice, there is the pain of being loved, and we welcome it."

I do not say she will cherish it tomorrow, because I want that to be her own meaningful discovery.

We rock and rock and the rain lets go all at once, spattering on my shoulders and back and buttocks. There is no beat between lightning and thunder; it is that close. And when it flashes I see little rivulets of mud begin to trace patterns around Alice's shoulders, and the empty place in my gut is full. We are one with each other and the charge of the storm and the now-full place thanks me for this elegant feast.

Tomorrow it will yawn open again, and I will pour myself a drink and project my mind back to the only part that matters.

When I arrive home from the general store with groceries, Alice is lurking dangerously close to my house. Walking down the side, away from the lake.

I catch up with her in front of the house, where I know my wife can't see, where I know she cannot wheel herself.

Alice tells me she was just walking by, and my wife called out to her from the porch and said, "Aren't you Alice? Wesley's little friend Alice?" Then she asked her up for a chat.

Anger is coiled tight and heavy in my chest, and a hot pressure of blood builds around my ears, but I breathe it down. Alice must not see my anger, because it will frighten her.

Alice is afraid of anger. I know.

She asks me why my wife is in a wheelchair, so I tell her about the accident, with a pulse drumming in the front of my head that says, *Never mind that.*

"Alice, you didn't tell her about the special part, right? Good girl."

I didn't even have to swear her to secrecy. I didn't have to say *let this be our little secret, Alice.* Alice has been trained from birth what not to say, what not to see, what not to repeat.

She is confused, I can see. Over little things, like why my wife calls me Wesley, and big ones, like why she seemed so real, when I described her as practically not existing. And obvious ones, like what my wife meant when she said I was a good man at heart, but don't be alone with me, no explanation as to why not.

I give her a big strong hug. If you had told me it would be the biggest mistake of the summer, I'd have done it again.

Alice needs hugging.

I kiss her forehead and tell her to run home, feeling loved.

I have matters to attend to.

My wife is on the porch overlooking the lake, where she says she cannot wheel herself without me. Another manipulation.

She has a blanket on her lap in that way she knows I hate. It makes her look like an old dried-up invalid. She is too young to look so old.

Her features are sharp and heartless, like an aging portrait of some nameless member of the aristocracy. She wields her wheelchair like a throne.

"Goddamn you," I say. My temples pound now, and I know it is a mistake to show her the extent of my upset but it's too late. There's no way out. "Where the hell do you come off scaring little girls by telling them I can't be trusted?"

She turns her eyes to me and they are blank and impassive, as usual, reminding me that it's not a result of the accident, the stillness from the waist down. It's the stillness inside.

"I suppose I was too late with this one," she says.

My heart flutters under the weight of the stress, and only barely is my anger contained. This is too quick a plunge back into reality, and I so need to be lowered slowly. It was so perfect. How dare she leave her fingerprints? How dare she?

I rock in her direction, half bent on lashing out, half attempting to prevent it. I grab the arms of her throne and push, and stumble forward, and as I hit my knees I hold tight to the chair. I do not let it roll toward the stairs. I do not.

"I need you," I say, and I rest my head in her lap. "Don't be angry with me. Nothing happened with the girl. Dammit, you know how much I need you."

She knows. But she likes to hear it just the same.

"Wesley," she sighs. And strokes my hair. "Poor, misguided Wesley. You have less self-discipline than any man I know."

The knock on the door is Mr. Cardboard. His hair is parted low on the side of his head, and combed to cover all that scalp. As though we'll be fooled into thinking it grows there.

I see by his face that he is not a happy man.

I step out and close the door behind me, just to be safe. Just to be sure my wife, who is all the way out on the back porch, cannot hear.

"My daughter is fourteen years old."

"I see. Is that all you came by to tell me?"

"Look, don't play games with me, you son of a bitch. I saw you hugging and kissing her."

He grabs me by my shirt, not seeing this as a big mistake. For one calculated moment I allow him his grasp on me.

"I gave Alice a hug and a kiss on the forehead. The type of thing a loving parent is known to do. You really should try that sometime. Children seem to have a universal appreciation of it."

He does not appreciate my casual attitude. It is not intended for his appreciation.

"Listen, you," he says. Oh bravo, I think. Good start. Powerful. "Anything you touch my daughter with, you'd better be prepared to lose."

And that is it, my point of no return. I crest the break where the water churns white and where even the miraculous restarting of a motor will not avert the fall.

I bring both arms up to break his grasp, spin him by the collar and slam him into my front door. Hard enough that he will feel the reverberation of the blow through his ribs, and he will feel it again tomorrow.

That is quite enough.

He gathers himself and leaves without comment.

I wheel my wife back into the house and sit on the porch with my feet up, awaiting the sheriff. My mind is quiet now, and I feel at peace. He will arrive soon, a man with a badge and tied hands. He will already have discussed the matter with Alice, who will have said I did nothing wrong. I will explain that Alice was upset to hear about my wife's accident.

She is a sensitive child. I gave her a little hug and a kiss on the forehead, so she would not have to be ashamed of her tears. And if her father had not grabbed me—on my property, I'll add—I would not have pushed him.

He will look into my eyes, aching to put me away, and tell me, with the arrogance of a man who holds no valid options, that I am to watch my step.

There is nothing more he can do.

The sheriff is forty-five minutes gone as I set my oars and cast my line into the water.

I am rocking with a gentle swell, my hat brim pulled down over my eyes, slipping into a meditative state.

I hear the motor and I am disturbed.

Not the tightness in my chest, it's not that kind of disturbance. Not blood pounding in my ears. That seems to carry with it a delicious sense of control.

This is a disturbance in the gaping hole of my gut.

As their boat skims by, its wake rocks my boat in unpredictable patterns. I dislike unpredictability.

Mrs. Cardboard holds her coiffure down with her hands as if it will blow away. Mr. Cardboard has a long flag of hair flapping off the side of his bare scalp.

They are taking her away before I can even say goodbye. I have so many things left to tell her. Important things that she will need to know. The hole in my gut is torn like a fresh wound, begging comfort and attention. A terrified child.

I must kiss away its tears.

I stand in my tiny boat, carefully balancing myself against the pitch and roll.

"Alice," I shout. "It's not you. It's them. You're not deaf, they're not saying anything."

I don't know if she can hear me.

Mr. Cardboard is waving his fist and shouting comments at me, which I presume to be unpleasant. But I can't hear him.

Alice waves goodbye, so I will know she still loves me.

"Don't forget me, Alice," I say quietly.

She doesn't need to hear that. She won't forget me.

I could say more, but the boat is gone.

WEDNESDAY MAN

*T*his time he lit candles and set them in place on the dusty altar, and again Suzanne was struck by the idea that he might not exist, or at least not outside this moment.

Where had he found candles? She could not imagine. And how old must they be? For a moment she imagined that they were simply available to his need, like loaves and fishes.

She would be able to see him more clearly this time, by their light, and the old chapel as well.

The pews were piled against one wall, covered in tarps and old lumber. The windows, which were plywood outside, showed remnants of thick, yellowish glass, targeted and shattered over and over again by the beer bottles of the restless local youth. An ancient confessional stood in one corner, curtained in cobwebs.

Suzanne turned to study it and was startled by a statue at her left shoulder, a woman with eyes turned to heaven, aging gold paint peeling from her plaster robe.

"Is that the Virgin Mary?" She asked this softly, but her voice seemed to offend the stillness.

He smiled. It was a gentle smile, as smiles always seemed to be on him. He said he supposed it was.

"You mean she was—here? All this time?" Before, there had been no candles, no way of knowing that the Virgin Mary watched.

He laughed. "I think she might have been looking the other way," he said, and pointed to the ceiling with his thumb.

Then he took a step toward Suzanne, and her stomach tightened uncomfortably, but she wanted him to take another.He did.

He put his arms around her and she buried her face against his chest.

He was so thin. So tall and so young. So different in her arms. She had expected him to look strange when naked, he was so thin. But from what little she had been able to see, his body was taut and reed-like, oddly graceful.

He looked like a man who might play a musical instrument, and play it well, but she had no way of knowing if he did.

She stood on her toes and stretched up to kiss him, and he laid her down on the cool wooden floorboards, again.

He sat up and put on his jeans after a time, then got up and began to wander.

Suzanne picked up his shirt and wore it. The tails came down almost to her knees. She had to roll the cuffs four turns.

Jeff's shirts, in contrast, always fit like they were her own, which seemed a shame. She liked the feel of a big man's shirt, a shirt to be lost in, and she knew that if she could see herself, she would like the look of it as well.

He stood at the confessional, and knocked cobwebs down with his handkerchief, and she came up behind him and ran her hands around to his smooth, narrow chest. A mouse ran by her foot and she did not jump.

He turned and kissed her, then slid into the confessional and drew the torn curtain behind him.

He asked if she had anything she would like to confess.

A few weeks ago she could have said no with a reasonably clear conscience, but there was no point in telling him what he already knew.

She stepped into the booth and heard him slide open the little door between them. She felt awed, as she always did with him, as though drawn to each moment by calling. The feeling was so immense that she sought to knock it back down.

"Should I say, 'Bless me, Father, for I have sinned'?"

"I hope you won't."

"What should I say?"

"I wouldn't know that."

Suzanne fell silent in wondering.

Her first temptation was to tell him about her abortion. She had not told anyone except Elaine. It had been so many years ago, it seemed by rights it should be gone, but it was never gone. It had been her first night with Jeff. He had asked her if she used birth control, in advance, the way a responsible man should, and she had lied and said she did, because she didn't want him to stop. At first she didn't tell him because everything was too new between them. She didn't think their love would survive that truth. Later she didn't tell him because she couldn't explain why she hadn't told him sooner.

She opened her mouth and said half the word "I," then shut down again. If she told him that, he would know something about her. She would share only those things that happened to her on the inside.

"Sometimes when I wake up in the morning—well, all the time, lately—I can't make myself get up. I just don't want to do it. I know I have this day in front of me, and I don't want it. You know what it feels like? It feels like a dead calm, like when you're sailing a ship, and you hit a glassy stretch. Nothing moves. But I don't think that's what it really is."

Suzanne's words came back as fresh news, surprising her.

"I've decided it's fear. I'm afraid of starting the day, but it feels like boredom, because I don't feel things. Can you imagine having a panic attack without even knowing it?" She heard nothing from his side. "That was a pretty strange confession, wasn't it? Do you feel things?"

"That depends on what there is to feel," he said.

"Now, don't make a joke out of it."

"I didn't mean it that way at all." His voice sounded serious. Hurt, even. "I'm pretty good at feeling anger. I don't know much about fear."

Suzanne could not imagine him angry. He seemed slow and deliberate, with a calm, open face.

She stepped out of the booth and pulled back the curtain on his side, and sat down in his lap. With her head on his shoulder she drew herself tightly against him, wishing for a way to be closer still.

There is a reaching, she knew, to that kind of closeness. A hungry reaching.

It is never satisfied. There is never enough.

She woke up on the grass, behind the chapel, and he was beside her. She could only assume he had carried her there in her sleep, and she never asked.

They lay under the circle of oak trees at the far edge of the old cemetery. He was still bare-chested, she was still wearing only his shirt.

She asked if he was cold, and he lowered his face until his mouth almost touched hers, and said no, and kissed her.

It crossed her mind that they were outdoors, where they could be seen, though it wasn't often that anyone wandered these grounds at night. She could not find it in herself to be concerned.

He lay on his back then, and they watched the stars through the dappling of leaves overhead.

Suzanne had always wondered how six oak trees had managed to grow in such a perfect circle. Had they been planted that way? If so, why?

"Do you ever think about the fact that space goes on forever?" he said.

"Well, no. I mean, does it? How can anything go on forever?"

"But that's just it," he said, "space isn't anything, it's nothing. It's just the nothing between stars. How can nothing end? Because if it ends, then what's on the other side?"

Suzanne thought about that until she hit the boundaries of her mind and the whole idea tangled back on itself again.

"I guess you're right."

"Will you be here next Wednesday?"

"I think so. I mean, yes. I will."

"Good."

"I guess I should give you your shirt back."

"I guess."

They made love again, and she gave him the shirt.

Jeff's car was in the driveway when she got home. She walked in the door calling his name as though it was a question.

"Hi, Suze," he called from the bedroom.

"You're home early."

"No, I'm not. It's after midnight."

The clock on the bedside table said twelve-seventeen. Next Wednesday she would have to wear a watch.

"Did you go jogging?" She was dressed in sweats; it was an easy question. "Where did you go?"

Suzanne sat on the edge of the bed and pulled off her running shoes. "All the way across town. Then up that half-mile hill to the old chapel." She was sorry to have said it. She had intended to make it sound like an innocent place to go, but now she felt it would have been better not to mention it at all.

"You *jog* up that? My god. Your heart must be ready to burst when you get to the top."

"No. My heart is stronger when I get to the top."

She peeled off her sweat suit, feeling the question in the air, wondering if it really hung as close and heavy as it seemed.

Last week she'd gotten home before Jeff, with plenty of time to adjust. Still, when he'd come in, it felt as though he'd turned on the lights in a comfortably dark room, leaving her squinting and feeling invaded.

Now, coming home to him like this, she felt an irritation, like that of a child rousted suddenly from sleep.

"I ran into Elaine, and we went out for a cappuccino. I really didn't know it had gotten so late."

She slid into bed beside him, and he put his arms around her, and he felt strange. Too short, too broad around. Nineteen years and now he felt unfamiliar.

He rarely held her anymore, but he held her that night, maybe sensing that he might soon be out of chances.

He sat in the dirt beside her, facing down the slope, his knees drawn up to his chest.

Suzanne picked up little bits of gravel and bounced them across the rotted wooden walkway to the chapel's back door.

A floodlight on a timer was aimed at the chapel. To discourage vandalism, she assumed. It backlit the cross on the roof, which stood out in eerie relief against the black sky, a movie scene with cinematography bigger than life. It cast a shadow for their cover.

The days were getting longer, which concerned her, yet seemed to be a problem with no solution.

"If you live right here in town" she said, "why have I never seen you on the street?"

Of all the questions Elaine had asked, it was the only good one.

"I don't know."

"Well, at least we have our stories straight."

"How's that?"

"Nothing."

She had answered every one of Elaine's questions with "I don't know", including the why questions.

Maybe there was no mystery to it, no answer. Maybe she hadn't seen him on the street because she just hadn't.

Unless he only existed on Wednesday nights.

"Have you told anybody?" She was edging toward a confession, and he seemed to notice.

"No. Have you?"

"I got into a position where I had to tell my friend Elaine, but I didn't tell her much." She wished she hadn't called Elaine by name. Now he knew she had a friend named Elaine. Now he knew an external detail about her.

"Was she shocked?"

"Yes and no. Not on balance. But she was shocked at the church part." She couldn't see him well but he looked as though he was smiling.

"You were too, at first," he said.

And she remembered that—it was true, though it seemed foolish, looking back.

He had asked her if she believed in going to hell, and she had said no, she didn't. Then he'd asked, if she did believe in going to hell, though, did she think she'd go for what she did, or for where she did it? She said she supposed she would go for what she did, and he said, then it doesn't much matter where, does it?

"She was shocked that I don't know your name." Suzanne fell into a silence which seemed to reverberate.

"Do you want to know my name?"

"No." It came out too fast, too adamant. "No, let's leave well enough alone."

"But I never know what to call you," he said, "unless I call you 'Beautiful'."

Suzanne laughed and shook her head. "Thanks, it's a nice thought. But no. It sounds too much like one of those Fifties beach party movies with Frankie Avalon."

"I don't think I ever saw one of those," he said, sounding apologetic, and then she knew why not. It formed a bad reminder, and she wished she hadn't invited it.

It made her wonder if he had ever tried to guess her age. She might pass for forty, but she wasn't, and never would be again, and he might be as old as his late twenties, but that was wishful thinking.

"What do you want me to call you?"

"Nothing," she said. "Nothing at all. It's all those words that I'm trying to get away from."

They sat quietly for a time, and Suzanne watched something that looked like a small bird flutter in and out of the beam of the floodlight. Then she saw that there were several, and couldn't decide if they were tiny birds or enormous insects.

She leaned into him enough to nudge his shoulder with her own. "What are those things?"

"Bats."

"Bats?"

"Bats. Little bats. They hunt insects in the light."

"Oh."

"They're harmless. You don't have to be afraid of them."

"I'm not."

"Are you okay?"

"Pretty much."

"Do you want to go back inside for awhile?"

She looked closely at her watch but couldn't make it out. "I think I need to go home."

"Okay."

He put his arms around her and she lay back down on the ground and pulled him down with her and held him until long after she knew she must be late.

Suzanne stepped out onto the terrace because she didn't know Jeff was there, and once she saw him she couldn't justify going back in again.

She sat down with her iced coffee, put her feet up on the railing, and gave the appearance of looking out at the ocean.

It was Wednesday, and Jeff had taken the night off from his little-theater duties, because, he said, they weren't spending enough time together. The more she'd argued, the more he'd insisted.

Now she felt restless, as though she were being kept waiting, even though she'd decided hours ago that she wouldn't be able to go.

It was almost eight o'clock and still reasonably light. The days were still getting longer, another progression over which she had no control.

A flock of Pacific brown pelicans fished just off the coast, circling in the air, then stalling, diving, and bobbing up from the water with clusters of smaller birds close by, hangers-on for leftovers.

Jeff was reading the paper but seemed to be watching her from the corner of his eye.

"Says here they're going to restore the old chapel. They formed a committee, and they're planning a fundraiser next month to hire a caretaker. So it doesn't get trashed again."

"Mmm."

"We should go up there sometime."

"No thanks. I jog up there all the time. I've seen it enough."

"Want to go to a movie tonight? There's two good things playing in Oak Park."

Suzanne tipped her glass back and drank the rest of her coffee, rattling the ice. "Awful long drive."

He folded the paper and tossed it down on the terrace floor. "What's wrong, Suze?"

"Nothing. Nothing's wrong."

"What *do* you want to do? You just want to go jogging, don't you?"

"No. Not tonight." And it was true, she didn't. Not with Jeff loose, wondering where she was. "I don't feel like doing much of anything."

Jeff got up, walked to the railing, and slammed it with the palm of his hand. "Dammit, Suze, I wish I knew what was wrong."

"If wishes were horses," she said, and set her glass down harder than she had intended.

"What?"

"If wishes were horses. That's what my mother used to say if I wished for anything."

"Right. Well. I never liked your mother, anyway." Jeff sat back down beside her and tried to look into her eyes. "I feel like we don't know each other anymore."

He seemed hurt when she laughed out loud.

"That is not how I see the problem," she said.

"Well, then, why don't you tell me how you see the problem, Suzanne? Maybe that would be a start." His words sounded clipped and anxious.

She turned to face him and said, "The way I see it, Jeff, we know each other too well."

His face seemed to soften and fall, as if he was suddenly low on air. "I don't know how to fix *that.*"

"Me neither," she said, and went back inside.

He lay against her on a wool blanket, on the creaky wooden floor, naked and spent, running his fingers along her face.

He said, "I missed you last week," the first words spoken that night.

She said nothing, but wove her fingers into the back of his thick black hair, held tightly, and pulled his face down to hers.

His gentleness disappeared. He shifted wordlessly to match her intensity, and he tried to roll on top of her again but she moved away.

She sat up and put on his shirt. It was her favorite one, with the tiny red pinstripes. She wandered indirectly to the confessional without bothering to button the shirt, and stepped inside.

She wasn't sure if she was trying to talk to him or to get away from him, but a moment later she heard him settle on the other side.

The little door slid open. She waited for him to ask what was wrong, prepared with an angry response. He didn't ask.

"I know you better"—She had started to say, than I know my husband, but he hadn't been told she had one, and might not want to be told now. —"than I meant to."

Then she sat quietly, wondering what he would say. It seemed strange to imagine that he would understand, because she didn't know him at all, but she felt he did understand, without words, and that was just the problem.

He came out a few minutes later, and knocked quietly on her side of the partition, and she opened the curtain, and he came in. He dropped to his knees in front of her, and she wrapped her arms and legs around him, and felt his cheek press down against the top of her head. They stayed that way for the longest time because, she believed, he knew better than to want to let her go.

She ran into Elaine in the middle of a Thursday afternoon.

Suzanne's arms were full of packages. She had been shopping for clothes, noticing that it didn't help as much as it used to.

Elaine said, "From the look on your face, I would say that it's over." And then, "Come on, I'll buy you a drink."

It worked out to two drinks and lunch, and at no time did Elaine ask why it was over, only when she'd made the decision.

It hadn't exactly been a decision, but Suzanne had spent three Wednesdays sitting on the terrace, in the exquisite silence of Jeff's absence, wondering if the Wednesday Man was waiting at the chapel, or if he knew enough not to bother.

The drinks went to her head far more than two drinks ordinarily might. As they left the restaurant, the sun was too bright. Suzanne stood on the sidewalk, her eyes squinted almost shut, and fumbled for her sunglasses. That was when she saw him.

He walked slowly to match the pace of the little girl whose hand he held. A young woman walked at his side, pushing a baby stroller. A tiny woman, too young, too pretty. He looked taller beside her, taller even than she'd remembered him.

His head swiveled around, and his gaze snagged on hers, and she knew absence had taught them nothing of letting each other go.

Then he looked away.

Elaine took hold of her elbow and said she looked as though she was about to faint, but she answered that she was fine and drove home alone with her packages, and had another drink.

Jeff came home at eight and found her on the terrace. It was almost dark. The days were getting shorter now, when there was no reason why they should.

He stood behind her, one hand on each shoulder, and said, "Suzanne, are you having an affair?"

Relieved to be looking at an ocean full of pelicans and not Jeff, she said, "No."

"But you were. Right?"

And she said *yes*, because it was too late anyway to think she could say something different.

"But it's over? It's absolutely over?"

"Yes. It's absolutely over."

"I need to know who it was, Suzanne. Who was it?"

She stood and turned to face Jeff, put her arms around his neck and looked into his eyes, because if she hadn't he would never have believed her, and told him she didn't know.

DIOGENES JONES

*H*er first, familiar impulse was to cry.

Then, glancing over to the passenger seat, she noticed that the gun was not pointed at her. The hitchhiker simply held it across the palm of his hand, respectfully, like some once-living thing. His face seemed soft and calm.

"You see this?" he said. "It's the only thing I got left to sell. Smith and Wesson. Three fifty-seven. Twenty bucks and it's yours. I need the money."

She couldn't handle stress. Not now. Her gut offered up a white flag of surrender, like the first time she tried to jog after the flu. It's either in you or it isn't.

Rosie shook her head softly. "Bad karma, you know? What would I do with a gun?"

"Hell, you could turn around and sell it for two hundred. More." His long, oily hair hung across his face, obscuring his profile. His voice cradled the desperation of the salesman who can't afford to blow one crucial deal.

"Look. Here's twenty. If you need it that bad. Keep the gun." She held the bill across the seat, motioned with it.

He turned his face to the window. "No charity." He slipped the bill out of her hand and into the pocket of his shredded jeans, opened her glove compartment and left the gun inside.

"Up there. 46 east. That's where I get off."

They rode in silence until she pulled onto the shoulder.

"God go with you," he said, and slammed the door.

She watched him walk for a moment, then eased back onto the highway. "He'd better. Especially now that I'm armed."

She comforted herself with the thought that it probably wasn't loaded. She preferred not to open the glove box to look.

She sat with her back against the clay-colored hill, miles, it seemed, above the Pacific Ocean, looking across narrow, deserted Highway 1 to the cliff she'd decided not to jump off. For now.

Beside her the old Chevy sat with two of its tires dead flat. Another tire gleamed with the heads of screws she'd never seen in the road, but it miraculously held air. In her hand lay the gun.

If I was smart, she thought, I'd cross the highway and throw it into the ocean. Now, before I do something stupid. Of course, if I was smart, I'd be home with the covers over my head. I wouldn't have pretended I could drive faster than my pain.

Martin, no stranger to the AA program, had once taught her the difference between normies and the diseased. "If a normie gets a flat tire, he calls Triple A. One of us gets a flat tire, we call suicide prevention. You may not have the alcohol thing, Rosie, but in your heart you're one of us."

Maybe. But at another time, it might just be a walk to a telephone. A long walk, but a walk, no more. But not in the face of so much loss. It was a joke, almost, but a bad one. Why can't things happen one at a time?

With the unfairness of life spinning in her brain like a one-car accident, Rosie climbed to her feet and aimed on the Chevy. She expected a click. The dry fire of an unloaded gun. Instead she got an explosion. A brain-numbing moment of hearing loss. A jolt through her hands, arms, right down through her feet. A kick that raised the shot. It tore through the windshield, not with a neat hole, as expected, but shattering the glass and dispersing it, leaving no square inch unharmed, sending seat stuffing flying.

Rosie swallowed hard, chastened and intimidated by her own sudden power. Then, seized by the pure satisfaction of the act, she fired two more rounds. One missed completely, the other destroyed the grill and blew out the core of the radiator. Steam coiled up to the sky, and brownish-green coolant puddled in the dirt.

She squeezed the trigger three more times. Three dry clicks. The moment was gone. One beautiful, expensive moment of release, which she knew she should have enjoyed more while it lasted.

She heard a slight noise and turned. A tall man stood on the highway behind her, an old man whose appearance belied his age. He wore jeans and a denim jacket, white shirt and brushy white flattop haircut, and showed fresh, colorful tattoos at his throat and beneath his rolled jacket sleeves. He carried a heavy pack with a bedroll on his back. He raised his hands in mock surrender.

"I didn't say a word."

"Where the hell did you come from?"

"Just walking through. Just thought I'd let you exhaust your rounds before I tried to pass."

"Walking through where? There's nothing in that direction."

"Beg to differ, madam, though you have the gun. San Luis Obispo is in that direction."

"San Luis Obispo is a hundred miles from here."

"I didn't say it would be a short walk."

She looked from the old man, to the gun in her hand, to the steaming leftovers of her old Chevy, and laughed. It was that or cry, and she was sick to death of crying. It's all she'd been doing for days.

"I'd give you a lift, except—"

"Except you just murdered your car." He set his pack in the dirt, approached the Chevy and squatted down to peer at the ventilated radiator. "Right through the heart. I hope you never get that angry with me."

"I'm not angry."

He raised his eyebrows. "Mind if I ask the automobile's opinion?"

"I'm depressed."

"I hope you never get that depressed with me."

"Shit. Now how am I going to get home?"

"Well, dear, at the risk of sounding like your mother, you should have thought of that before you killed the car."

He shouldered the big pack and headed south. Rosie watched him for a hundred feet or so, then he stopped and turned back.

"I'd move along if I were you. Before this is noticed."

"Why? Is it against the law to murder your own car?"

"That depends. Did you shoot it with a licensed gun?"

"I'm moving."

She crossed the empty highway to the cliff and brought her arm back in a great windup, already picturing the murder weapon flying, spinning, crashing on the rocks below. A hand grasped her wrist.

"My, you are an impulsive little critter."

"I don't want it. Look what happens."

"If you want to throw hundreds of dollars away, throw it my way." He held out his hand to receive the gift.

Rosie stared at the gun. Hundreds of dollars. A ticket home. There would likely be a gun dealer in San Luis Obispo. She stuck it in the waistband of her jeans.

"Damn. I knew you'd show some brains sooner or later. Later would have been nice."

He lay beside her in his sleeping bag, a few yards off the highway in the redwoods. She pulled his blanket tighter around herself. It wasn't enough. But it was more than she would have had without him.

Tomorrow would be a workday. What would Bossman think when she didn't show? His first reaction would not be anger; she was too damned dependable to afford him that luxury. He would worry, a small comfort.

Her voice betrayed the shivers. "I don't even know your name."

"Glenn."

"Rosie. Jones."

"Get serious."

"What's wrong with Rosie Jones?"

"Rosie Jones is nobody's real name. It's a perky talk show host. Or a brave, plucky heroine in a dimestore novel."

"You're a great comfort, Glenn."

He sat up, sleeping bag and all, and lit a cigarette. They watched the moon, a great yellow thing, almost full. It hovered on the horizon, sending a trail of itself toward them, over miles of water. She watched his cigarette glow in the dark.

"What are you angry about, Rosie Jones?"

"I got dumped."

"Ah. Love. That explains a lot."

"I don't get why it keeps turning out the same way."

"What way is that?"

"He didn't love me. I mean, not the way I love him."

"Maybe you ask too much."

"I just want someone to love. Is that too much?" The tears came back, hot, irresistible, unwelcome, yet a relief to slip into. Sobs mixed with shivers in her voice. "I'm cold."

"Yes, dear, that's very metaphoric. Look, don't take this the wrong way." He hugged her with both arms around her shoulders. "I'm too old and otherwise disinclined. Trust me." He rubbed her shoulders briskly for warmth. "I am about to reveal the great secret of the universe, Rosie Jones, so I hope you're paying attention: You will always get exactly what you ask for."

Her body jerked up straight, and she pulled away from his grasp. "I didn't ask for this."

"You did. You said, 'I just want someone to love.'"

"Right."

"And do you love this guy, this . . ."

"Martin. Yes. A lot." Rosie pressed her eyes shut and clenched her teeth against the chattering. "Guess I should have asked for someone to love me."

Silence. Then his arms around her again, warm and enveloping. "*I* love you, Rosie."

"Oh, shit, I was afraid of this. Look, Glenn—"

"Rosie, you fool, I'm attempting to make a point."

"Oh. You mean, a man might just be *saying* he loves me?"

"Rose, you are thick. I'm saying if you just ask for someone to love you, be prepared to end up with a golden retriever. Or me. You are asking far too little. And getting it, I might say. Look, take out a sheet of paper and number from one to ten."

"Huh?"

"Figuratively speaking. Now, start every sentence with the word 'gimme'. The universe responds well to such directness. Gimme mutuality. Gimme a man who can actually express an emotional thought. Gimme a man who won't head for the hills like a scared bunny when things get good. Jump in anytime, dear."

"You think a guy like that exists, Glenn?" A moment of silence. "Well? Do you?"

He flicked his disposable lighter, and the flame illuminated his intricate face. "Need a light, Diogenes?"

They hitchhiked more than half the distance home, and arrived south of the Big Sur coast, where the highway flattened to sea level and hosted a series of small coastal towns.

In a little pub on the Main Street of somewhere, Rosie watched Glenn lean over a pool table and cruise into his fourth game, watched it dawn on the faces of the men around him that they had made an error in judgment.

She tried to shake the feeling of inhabiting someone else's world. Why, she wasn't sure. She'd left the house yesterday determined to abandon her own.

Familiar heartache rattled at the edges but did not try to come in. How could it? It would only be in the wrong place. It pleased her to pause where the hurt couldn't reach. For now.

Glenn lined up a difficult shot, banked the cue ball and sank two. His opponent winced, then sidled up to Rosie.

"A looker like you could do better."

"I'll ignore that."

Glenn's head came up from his shot, and a smile spread on him, looking warm and at home. "I think the man was talking to me, sweetheart."

She returned a not-too-sharp sarcastic glance and kissed Glenn briefly on the lips. She was only following orders.

"Look adoringly at me," he'd said. "Flirt with all the guys but make it clear they can't hold a candle to me. You're a class act, but you're taken."

"You're a sick man, Glenn."

"I know exactly what I'm doing. I am going to show you what true pool hustling is about. And you are going to help me attract enough attention to do it. Trust me."

"I never trust a man who says trust me."

"Good rule. Make an exception."

He sank the eight ball and offered another game. The young sucker's visible pride rose up. Everybody was watching now. The old man had to be brought down.

Halfway through the game, the sucker spoke up. "How'd you get so lucky with cute little Rosie here?"

"Rosie who?"

"Your girlfriend. Right there."

"Did she tell you her name was Rosie?" He sank three balls. "Her real name is Diogenes Jones. But you can call her Lady Di." He leaned until his whole body stretched at a crazy angle across the table. Sank the ten. "She's traveling under an alias. Wanted by the law."

The young man turned to Rosie, looking surprised and impressed. "No shit. What for?"

Glenn sank the eight ball and smiled. "Vehicular manslaughter."

"So, how'd you get so lucky anyway?"

"Fortune has nothing to do with it, my good man. In love, that is. In pool, I'm just a lucky son of a bitch. Double or nothing?"

When the pride she playacted felt too real, Rosie excused herself and wobbled to the ladies room. She set her Corona bottle on the dirty bank of sinks, stared at herself in the mirror and splashed water on her face. When had she last been drunk? Long before Martin, that was certain.

She suddenly missed a handful of items she'd carelessly left in the car. A metal flashlight her father had given her for emergencies. Her favorite Peter Gabriel cassette. An old satin baseball jacket she'd left behind the seat. She felt stripped somehow, as though too much of what defined her was left behind. For the moment it didn't matter that more of her identity waited at home. What she'd lost seemed more important.

She dried her face on a paper towel and slid back out into the pub, running smack into Glenn at the door.

"Want to turn that cursed murder weapon into a hundred bucks? I met a guy who's interested."

"He'll pay a hundred cash?"

"He'll pay two hundred cash. You'll give me half for cutting the deal. Then we'll get out of here, fast. Before these suckers find some bullets."

At the Sea Cliffs Motel, in a room with two double beds, Rosie sprawled against Glenn on his, fully dressed on top of the covers, both too drunk to remove their shoes and clean up for sleep.

"These tattoos are fresh. Aren't they?"

"Relatively. They were a present to myself for my seventieth birthday."

"You know, the ladies in that bar liked you. You've still got something. Bet when you were young, you had any woman you wanted."

"Yes. Every one I wanted."

He rolled onto his back and threw his arm around her shoulder. The feeling in her stomach was back, that shaky emptiness undermining a healthy body. *Home*, it clearly demanded. Failing that, it accepted Glenn's arm as a down payment.

He lit a cigarette one-handed. She watched his smoke curl lazily toward the ceiling.

"Anybody still make passes?"

"Oh, a year or so ago, there was a sweet young thing. But it'd been too long for me. What you don't use, you lose."

"You couldn't, huh?"

"I was hoping to remain vague and genteel."

"Oh. Sorry."

She rested her head on his chest, comforted by the size of him. "So, you'd probably rather I didn't, then."

"I would definitely rather you didn't, Di. This was a sweet young male thing."

"Oh. Oh, shit. I *am* stupid."

"Supremely. But it's okay. Just get a good night's sleep." He kissed the side of her forehead.

Stranger than her feeling of jealousy was the fact that it didn't feel strange.

They stood outside the door to her apartment, the key in her hand. The door across the hall opened, and a middle-aged woman stepped out.

"My god. I'm seeing a ghost."

"Hi, Viv. What, you know this guy?"

"You, Rosie. We thought you were dead. I mean, they found your car up the coast. All shot up."

"Oh. That. Well . . ."

She stumbled for words and Glenn took over. "The reports of her death have been slightly exaggerated."

"Yeah. What he said."

"I'll have to call Martin and tell him you're okay. He's been beside himself."

Rosie exchanged a look with Glenn as they stepped inside.

"I thought Martin cut your walking papers."

"He did. But you know how men are."

"Now, now, Di. Keep up the search."

He disappeared for most of the day, arriving back in the evening with a bottle of rum, just when she believed he was gone.

"Martin called. I told him I'm moving on to someone new."

"Hope you were kidding."

"Half."

It was a lie, actually, but a small one. He *would* call. She *would* say that.

He passed the bottle, and in the silence she heard it, the drawing away. Heard and felt it. It's always there, evident at twenty paces. You only think it's not, when you don't want to know.

"Rosie. You're making a big mistake."

"You called me Rosie."

"Believe me, kid, if your list leaves room for me, you need a longer list. Or a nice golden retriever."

"Glenn?"

"Yes, Di?"

"Why do you live like this? Why don't you ask for better?"

"Who's to say there is anything better?"

"Oh, come on. Walking and hitchhiking and hustling and sleeping out in the cold. You're not a kid anymore. Some nights you must want better."

"Some nights. Look, Di. There's an old saying. Those who can, do. Those who can't, teach. Just because I don't take my advice doesn't mean you shouldn't."

"Right. Whatever."

"Now you're angry."

"No. I'm not. I'm going to bed."

"Di?"

"Yes, Glenn."

"Just do the opposite of what I do. Hold out for more."

"Yeah. Whatever."

They slept in her bed together, and she couldn't claim surprise at waking up alone. She reached out to his pillow for the note.

Dear D., Good advice is all I'm worth. I hope it was worth your VCR, because that's what it cost you. I almost couldn't do it to you, though I wouldn't think twice with anyone else. But you had to learn. Nobody wants to be saved. Save yourself.

Martin called at nine-thirty. She let the machine pick up. Halfway through his impassioned display of relief she unplugged the phone at the jack. She wished Glenn could see. She'd hold her imaginary lantern aloft and say, "I'll take that light now."

Next time Martin called, she'd pick up. And, not to make a liar of herself, she'd say she was ready to move on to someone new. She wouldn't mention it was a golden retriever unless he asked. And he probably wouldn't ask.

THE KEEPER

*W*hen I was thirteen and Kenny was sixteen, that was a good year. I could still take him for walks. He ran off a lot but he never tried to hurt anybody.

I always made him wear a roll of toilet paper on a string around his neck. That was my own invention, and believe me, it made things a lot easier. I always had something handy to wipe his chin.

Life was simple until Mrs. Wexler caught up with us on Andrews Avenue and said, "Lawrence, you are nothing but a litterbug." After that I made Kenny wear a plastic bag tied to his belt loop, for the used paper. Problem was, it took two hands to open the damn thing, and the minute I let go of his wrist, he was off.

It's amazing, really, how someone so uncoordinated could move so fast. Half the time his feet would flop over so he'd be running on his ankles. Likely as not he'd bang into something or just fall down. With his wrists all doubled over he'd wave his arms like he was bringing in a plane.

But he was a son of a bitch to catch.

One day we were waiting for a light at the corner of E Street, and this kid I'd never met called him a vegetable.

"Takin' the vegetable for a walk?" That's what he said.

His ass was mine. He got one good shot to my eye and then I was on him, knees on his shoulders, hitting him in the face. By the time he said *uncle* you could hardly make out the word.

I let him up and looked around. I knew Kenny had run off, but I hoped I'd see which way he'd gone. He was nowhere. It was after six and I was hungry. But I couldn't go home without him. *Where's Kenny? I lost him.* It wasn't good enough.

So I pounded the streets, asked neighbors if they'd seen him go by. Now and then I'd stop and look in a shop window. Watch my eye swell up.

Finally a cop car pulled up behind me. That big cop with the red hair. I never remembered his name, but I knew him.

"This what you're looking for?" he said. He had Kenny in the back. Nobody had wiped his chin for an hour. He was a mess. "You'll have to keep your brother on a tighter leash."

"It won't happen again, sir. I promise."

But it happened every day. He knew it and I knew it.

When I dragged in the door, my mom took one look at me and said nothing. It was the end of a merciful progression which had started years before with, "Lawrence, my god, what happened?" Within a few months it became, "What was it this time?" which faded almost unnoticed into, "What do you care what they say about Kenny? He doesn't care."

That day no comment, the kindest comment of all.

I put Kenny straight into his room in the basement.

When I'd locked the door she said, "It's getting harder, isn't it?"

I said it was fine.

I was fourteen by Christmas, and the first person awake. I was on the run to let Kenny up from the basement; I figured we'd watch Howdy Doody until my mom woke up. But at the second-floor landing I stopped. There was a strange man at the bottom of the stairs. My guts went cold and I wanted to run, but I couldn't think to where.

He was staring at the pictures on the wall. Me and Kenny when we were little. In his arms was a half-grown Airedale pup. When he looked up at me, he didn't seem surprised.

I took two steps down to him, because I knew then that it was my father. He looked back at the pictures in a sort of a trance. I walked down and stood next to him, and the dog wiggled and reached for me and tried to lick my face. My father handed her off to me. She was almost too big to hold but I held her anyway.

"Merry Christmas, son," he said. His eyes darted up and before I could even follow them, I knew my mother was awake. She stood on the landing, her eyes wide, and for the first time I wondered how he got in. Did he still have a key?

"Edith," my father said.

She stood frozen a moment, then pulled her robe tight around her and flounced down the stairs. The puppy was squirming and kissing and about to slip. I wanted to be a kid at Christmas, happy I had her, but I was caught up in this quiet cross fire, like the issue from high-tension wires scattered on the floor at my feet.

As she scraped past us, I thought I heard her say, "Merry Christmas, Ed." She definitely said something, but muffled, not charitable enough to be fully delivered. She disappeared into the kitchen, and when I looked back, my father was almost at the door.

"Dad," I called, and he turned back. "Didn't you bring something for Kenny?"

His eyes rolled up to the ceiling like there was a cheat list up there for questions like that. His voice boomed loud, too loud, so the house didn't feel like Christmas. "What the hell good would it do to bring something for Kenny? Kenny don't know what you bring."

I watched the door long after he was gone.

I threw the ball across the yard for the pup, without regard to the fact that it was supposed to be Kenny's. Kenny liked to fetch, too, and I hadn't let him out yet. I'd taught Kenny the game with a little plastic blow-up ball, but he bit right through it, so I got him the hard rubber ball for Christmas. He couldn't have known it was his ball but he knew it was his game, and I could hear him pounding on the basement windows and throwing himself around down there.

I wanted a little more time with the pup, but she yipped and barked and wouldn't stop. My mother came out on the back porch and said that between the dog and my brother the neighbors would call the police, so I let Kenny out.

He went barreling across the back lawn, his arms out like he would give the pup a hug. Instead he tried to grab her with both hands around her throat. His wrists were always hooked in, though, like a spastic, and he missed with his left, but his right hand got a good hold. The puppy yelped and sank her teeth into his arm as I flying-tackled him onto the grass. We rolled over the dog but she was a tough little bugger, she jumped up and shook off and ran.

I pinned Kenny onto the grass and hit him. Over and over. Saying, "No! No!" every time. Finally my mother put a hand on my shoulder and said, "That's enough, Lawrence."

In the morning she called my father to find out where he got the dog, who still hid under the back porch. I tried to coax her out with food but it took me almost an hour to catch her. I carried her into the house the way my father had, dangling off my arm.

"Do I have to take her back?"

"No, Lawrence, but one of them has to go."

"Okay, fine," I said. "I'll take her back now."

I didn't cry until I got all the way under the back porch where nobody could see.

Kenny knew I didn't forgive him, so things got worse. He picked up a bad habit of sitting down in the middle of traffic when we crossed the street. He did it to get back at me, plus I think he liked the control of stopping traffic. It was the only control he had.

If I really pushed him to do something he'd wet himself. Then I had to take on laundry on top of everything else.

When I got tired of the new tricks, the walks stopped. Every day I'd go down and see him. Every day tell him, "If you want me to forgive you, this is a funny way to ask." But I knew he didn't understand my words. The lack of forgiveness, that he understood.

And then, just when I thought things couldn't get any worse between us, Belinda came along. I was walking her home from my house one night around dusk when she stopped under the streetlamp out front and asked for a kiss.

"By the time we get to my house," she said, "I won't dare."

I'd never kissed a girl before. I didn't know I wanted to kiss this one until I did. And then I knew I'd never stop wanting it, that I'd taken hold of something I would never let go of again. Or it had taken hold of me. I was so caught up that I heard the sound of breaking glass and never thought to wonder. Then I saw him out of the corner of my eye. There was no mistaking that motion. Nobody ran like Kenny. Belinda saw him, too, and screamed.

His face was bleeding, maybe from the basement window. The way he was waving his arms, he must have looked like a horror-movie creature to her. By then Kenny was like a dog that's been chained too long, meaner and uglier with every passing day.

Belinda ran, and Kenny took off after her, and I took off after Kenny. As he grabbed for her hair I caught him, spun him by the back of his shirt and threw him onto the sidewalk.

Next thing I remember I had both hands around his throat, screaming, "I'm *not* giving *this* one *away!*" over and over and over. Every time I said, "not" and "this" and "way" I slammed Kenny's head on the pavement.

When I looked up, Belinda was three blocks down, still running, and I knew I'd never see her again.

The doctor said I shouldn't feel guilty, because I probably hadn't done that much. He said if Kenny hadn't had skull fragments in his brain already, he might have jumped up and hit me back.

Then everybody started to say it. Mom and Aunt Edna and Grandma Keene. Then I had to hide under the back porch again, to not hear how they all said it. All except my father, who never showed. Even at the funeral, he never showed.

It took five weeks to find my father, because I couldn't bring myself to tell my mother I was looking.

I tracked him down through three abandoned jobs.

He answered his apartment door in boxers and a sleeveless T-shirt. I could tell I'd wakened him. As soon as he let me in he closed his bedroom door, and as he did, I saw someone roll over in his bed.

"I remember what happened to Kenny."

His defensiveness rose up so I could almost see it. I expected to feel like a weak little boy against it, but didn't.

"That was an accident," he said.

"Yeah, an accident." My voice was up. I wondered if it sounded scared to him. It sounded scared to me.

"Look, you're a fine one to talk," he said. "I'm not the one that killed him."

I don't remember telling my body to go into motion, but I hit him like a speeding train. I expected him to go down, like Kenny would have, like kids my own age.

He threw me off with one arm and slammed me into the wall. I came at him again, and he bounced me off the wall again. And again. Like he'd done to Kenny, only all my hits were lucky. I came up as myself.

I stayed against the wall, panting, staring him down. I wanted to kill him, and I know he saw that in my eyes.

"See?" he said. "You're just like your old man."

Before I sneaked up to my room, I stopped at the bottom of the stairs to look at the pictures. Sometimes when pictures are always there you don't see them anymore, until something makes you see.

The one that really hurt was a picture of me and Kenny, side by side. Before. We were both looking right into the camera, and his eyes were so clear. And his mouth was closed. I'd almost forgotten he used to look like that. I thought, that's my big brother.

Then I saw the hands. My father's hands on his shoulders. Even though my father wasn't in the picture, I knew it was him, touching Kenny.

I pulled the picture off the wall and smashed it against the banister. Again, that awful sound of breaking glass.

When my mother came running in I let it fall. She tried to put her arms around me, but I shook her off again.

I said, "I remember what happened to Kenny."

She said, "I didn't know you'd ever forgotten."

"Why didn't you do something?"

In the deadly silence that followed, I wondered how you break somebody's heart. Can you do it with words? Those words? I remembered the time she said my father broke her heart. I thought, I'm just like my old man.

"I did, Lawrence, just not in time. Can you forgive me for that?" I tried to run up to my room but she stopped me with words. "Can you forgive yourself?"

I sat down hard on the stairs. I said, "I just wanted to keep him where he'd be safe."

She said, "I know, honey," and then she took me up to my room and tucked me in, like a six-year-old, and kissed my forehead, and I didn't mind.

I asked her if I was anything like my father.

She said, "Not even a little bit. Why?"

"No reason." She headed for the door. "Mom? Can we get a dog?"

She said we'd talk about it in the morning.

NICKY BE THY NAME

*F*rancie: The day we buried my mother, Pop took us home from the funeral, changed into his gardening clothes, shuffled out to the backyard and proceeded to prune the roses. Mind you, the roses were well-pruned already. But in his mind I suppose they needed something, some measure of control.

I sat in my swing and watched him, still in my funeral dress, swinging at times, holding still with my toes pressed into the soft dirt at others.

He moved like a man twenty years older than he'd been the previous day, face cast down toward the soil. Now and then he'd take out a handkerchief and mop away some sweat I could swear wasn't there.

Nicky went straight up to his room, but Michael stayed down to give Poppa the usual grief. He still wore the black suit Poppa had bought him for the funeral. He looked like a man to me. I was so impressed. Poppa's head came up to address him, as one faces an adversary, never showing his back.

"Some god, huh Pop?"

I skidded to a stop on the swing and waited, waited for the

hackles to rise on Pop, to feel the barbs engage, but he just looked tired.

"The good often die young," he said, and made a show of going back to pruning.

Michael raised his voice out of proportion to the conversation, as though he was furious at Pop for not being furious. "Oh, that's great. Maybe I'll just be bad, then."

Pop was a humorless man. He didn't laugh, or even smile, but raised his lip in a sort of a sneer. "Maybe?"

"Fuck you, Pop," Michael shouted back, because Michael cussed when he was hurt. "Didn't you hear me, old man? I said fuck you, and fuck your god, too."

I waited for Michael to take his beating.

Nicky never got beatings and neither did I. Pop would have said it was because Michael gave cause, but it wasn't quite so simple. Pop beat Michael because Michael gave cause; Michael gave cause because Pop beat him. It was a chain, no one could find the ends, and no one held a link that seemed to want to give.

Michael liked beatings—that's what Nicky and I used to say, just to each other and to ourselves. He knew how to pull Pop's strings, get right up against the grain, and push and push until it was a matter of pride to our father not to back down. Then he'd throw it like the live grenade it was, he'd say, "Fuck you, old man."

Pop would make him cut his own switch. Now what fool would bring back a good one? Michael would, every time. He said if he brought back a wimpy one, Pop would just send him out again. I think it was partly that, but a pride thing too.

I'd watched him from the stairs once or twice, take his whipping, his face twisted with hate, like all that hate might override the pain, and he never cried, though you could see it would have been easy. When Pop let up he'd stand to face him, pants around his knees, and Pop would ask if he'd learned his lesson. "Fuck you, old man." And they'd go around again.

Second, third, fourth time, Pop would ask no questions and Michael would volunteer no insults, just walk away with his head high.

"After awhile his arm gets tired," is what Michael told me.

But that day, the day of Mom's funeral, Pop looked away from Michael's words and pruned roses. Michael stormed from the yard and down the street. Pop leveled me with the strangest of looks. It startled me. I thought he'd forgotten I was there.

"You know you're the woman of the house now."

I laughed, though I knew he wasn't kidding. He couldn't have been. Not Pop. "But I'm just a kid."

"You're the closest thing to a woman the family's got."

I was only nine years old. I'm not sure it was fair of Pop to foist womanhood on me like that. That he was fresh out of grown women was hardly my concern.

I slid around him at a run to find Nicky, to tell him the news, how Michael said *fuck you* to Pop and Pop didn't switch him.

Nicky was lying on his bed with his arms behind his head. His cat Harrison was curled up on his chest. He seemed kind of lost, so I just lay down beside him, and put my arms behind my head.

"Nicky, is Mom ever coming back?"

"Nope," he said, but I still didn't get it. I mean, I did, in my head, but not where it counts.

Pop never raised a hand to Michael again. I knew in my gut and in my heart that it was an insult, not a mercy, and I'm sure Michael knew it too, as though he was no longer worth the effort.

Michael tried and tried but the old strings were cut, and in time Michael found new sources for his beatings.

Michael: I hated being the son of a preacher and I hated being one of twins. In both cases nothing is really you and there's nothing that can't be, won't be, taken away.

Best thing could have happened was getting my forehead split open by that body shop man. Needed a bumper for my new Chevy, needed it for free, ended up with a tire iron across my eyebrow, but I got a few good licks in, too, before it was all declared.

I wouldn't get it stitched, just put a butterfly bandage on it and tried to avoid Pop, but it got infected, and the old man had to take me to the doctor.

Doctor said it was amazing it didn't kill me, and Pop said I was too ornery to die. And that's all there was to that, except my eyebrow stayed messed up, never quite matched right with itself, and that's why I say it's a good thing, because then nobody could fail to tell us apart, with one obvious exception.

How people could fail to see the difference I will never know, anyway, because Nicky wasn't too smart. I mean, he did better in school than me, but only because he paid attention, did his homework, stuff like that. And he didn't have much of a sense of humor. If people were clowning around or telling jokes he'd give this big, baboony smile, because he wanted to get it, but you could tell he didn't. To make him laugh out loud, somebody would have to, say, step on a rake and have the handle hit them in the face. He had terrible table manners and his room was such a mess you couldn't see the floor.

So when somebody thought I was just like my brother, I couldn't take it well. I grew my hair long, bought a leather jacket out of my own money, wore it with the collar up. Called Nicky my kid brother—because he was; nine minutes younger—and he had to know he wasn't free to tag along.

When I got the Chevy back together I took to cruising, staying out late, waiting for Pop to say something. But Pop treated me like a warm wind that blew right through him.

One thing he'd never stand for, though, and that's strong drink, as he called it. Wouldn't have it in his house. First time I came home smashed with a bottle of Jim Beam in my pocket, Pop flat out told me to leave and never come back.

I left all right, cut tire tracks in circles on the lawn, and took out a few neighbor's trash cans on the way down the street, and in my rearview mirror I saw Pop throwing clothes out my bedroom window onto the lawn.

And while I was driving, with no idea where to, for some reason I thought about that story I wrote and never showed anybody, about Mr. Mike and his talking dog. The one Nicky found and said was good, ought to be published, and I said fine, put your name on it and publish it. I didn't think he really would. But it ended up in that school magazine. Pop was so damn proud of Nicky. And I couldn't stop wondering, if my name had been on it, would he have been proud of me?

And then I got to thinking about my kid sister Francie, and how she got to live at home whatever she did, and how much Poppa loved Nicky, even though Nicky had no brains, no guts, no personality. Nobody home.

But Poppa thought the sun rose on Nicky, and it's no wonder.

I was only sixteen then, but I didn't set foot in town again until the night of our nineteenth birthday, and then I got it in my head that Nicky and I could celebrate. That I could take him out and get him drunk, show him what it meant to be a man, because I'd learned it pretty good by then.

I stopped off at a bar to get a little oiled, in case I had to deal with Pop, and I ran into two guys I knew from high school. And I got to buying them drinks, telling them all the things I'd done, a few of which I really had.

I guess they wanted to test me out, because they made me a bet concerning this guy they called Killer, bet me a hundred bucks I wasn't brave enough to burn him. They said it was a good bet, because even if I was brave enough I wouldn't live to collect their money.

I wouldn't have wasted my time, except I'd been having some trouble with the carburetor on my van, and I needed the hundred.

And by then I knew quite a bit about how to pull things and survive. So I struck up a game of pool with Killer, casually came around to asking if he had a taste for the white lady, and when he said he did I slipped out to my van, made up a little bag of pure baby powder, and sold it to him in a stall in the men's room for three hundred dollars.

Just before I slipped out, thinking it was all too easy, he took hold of my arm, said I should hang around while he tasted it, and then, a few drinks past the centerline, the fear of death seemed real close and clear. I broke and ran like hell.

He got hung up in some dancing couples on the floor, which saved me, and I got out the door and around my van, and lay on my belly underneath it, watching his feet move up and down the street, until he turned the corner. Then I came out and tried to start the van but it wouldn't go.

Normally I'm not one to panic. Maybe it was the old town, too much whiskey, who knows? I slipped down an alley and found a pay phone on the next street, phoned Nicky and asked him to come get me.

And then I crawled back under my van and waited for him, because I knew I'd see him come up, and I'd have to stop him from going inside the bar. The street was cold and wet on my belly and against my cheek, but that's the last thing I remember, so I must've passed out.

Looking back on my life so far, which I swear I really do from time to time, I wonder why Pop was always so quick to forgive Francie and Nicky, even for the big things. Sometimes I try to remember back to who I was and what I did when things went wrong between us, but it was all too long ago.

For all the bad things I've said about my brother Nicky, he thought well of me in spite of everything. I rely on that. I really do. I think it's most of what keeps me going now.

Francie: The night Nicky got killed was his nineteenth birthday. That means I was fourteen, and Michael, wherever he was, was nineteen and nine minutes. The phone rang after midnight. Pop was a heavy sleeper, and I'm not sure if he ever knew that part. He once slept through an explosion at the cement factory, and all the sirens that came after.

Nicky had an extension in his room, and I heard him pick it up. I put my ear against the wall, which was thin, and I heard most of what he said, only he didn't say much.

Just, "Yeah." And then, "Yeah," again. Then, "Where are you?" And, "Yeah, alright."

I watched out my window, which was on the second floor looking over the garage. I watched Nicky push Pop's car down the driveway, then jump in and coast as it picked up speed, and I wondered why he thought the car would wake Pop if the phone didn't.

Nicky had a girlfriend, Kate, and I figured she had a present for him that Pop wouldn't approve of, and all I could think was how mad Pop would be if he knew Nicky took the car.

He turned south out of the driveway, and the engine sputtered up and the headlights came on, and I thought, if Pop catches you. "You're a dead man, Nicky." Then I went back to bed.

The call came in about one-thirty, and woke me up again. I was alone in the house with Pop, and I knew that he would never answer it, but I had a bad feeling about this one, and I'd sooner have picked up a scorpion. After eleven rings I went into Pop's room and shook him awake, and he stumbled up and took it on the kitchen phone. All the color drained out of his face, and he said, "No. It's got to be Michael." Then he listened in silence for a few seconds, and finally he said, "Yes, I'll come down."

He thought I was too young to be in the house alone at night.

"I'll bring the car around," he said, and then he shuffled stiffly back a few minutes later, as though there had been several places to look. He called a cab without comment and sat by the window to wait.

It was raining again, and water streamed down the window, and the streetlight in front of the house threw a reflection of the torrent onto our father's face.

"What happened, Pop?" I said, because enough time had gone by, I could see he didn't plan to volunteer it.

"One of the boys got hurt, and I have to go identify the body."

The two parts of that sentence didn't seem to mesh, but I just fell quiet again.

Suddenly Pop felt like talking. "They said it's Nicky, but I know it's not, he had Nicky's ID, but Michael could have had Nicky's ID; that wouldn't surprise me a bit. Mistaken identity. Because nobody would want to hurt Nicky. He'd never give them cause."

As he rambled it struck me that he hadn't gone upstairs to check Nicky's room.

I talked him into letting me stay home. At first I sat in the window, picturing the rain reflected on my face. Then I went up to Nicky's empty room, and found the story, and read it again.

I'd first found it years ago, cleaning Nicky's room, which he used to pay me a buck to do to keep Pop off his back.

It was about this man in our neighborhood—Mr. Mike, we called him—and his dog Peppy, and how Mr. Mike trained the dog to say, "I want my Momma." That was true, I'd heard it. It wasn't clear, kind of howly, but you could make it out if you tried. Mr. Mike used to bet the kids an ice cream soda that they couldn't catch Peppy, because it was easier than walking him. And Nicky learned the trick after awhile, to turn away and pretend he didn't care, and the dog would come to him.

"How come nobody teaches us that?" he had written. "That if you chase what you want it only runs faster? And why is it that everybody, even orphans and dogs, cry that they want their momma? Why does everybody need one if everybody doesn't get one?"

When I first read it I cried, and I didn't stop for almost three days. Nobody understood what was wrong with me, because Momma had been dead two years, and how could I explain that it had only just hit me to cry?

I read it again. I tried to cry again. When I was sure it wouldn't work, I went back downstairs to the window and stared at the rain until the cab pulled up and Pop got out, pulling his collar up and hunching his shoulders as if that would keep his head dry.

He opened the front door and set his keys on the hall table, then stared at them like he didn't know what they were.

He said, "It was Nicky."

I said, "I know."

Michael came to town for the funeral. He wore faded Levis and white sneakers with holes in the toes, a black suit coat he'd borrowed from someone smaller than himself, and a narrow black tie.

He walked right up to Pop and said, "Pop," like it was a statement of fact, and Pop looked him up and down the way a man looks at a horse he thinks is overpriced.

"You look like a bum," Pop said, and walked off leaving Michael speechless.

Nobody cried except me.

Michael came to the house after the funeral, when Poppa was away at Aunt Eva's. I told him Pop might well kill him if he found him in the house, but he just laughed, and got

Poppa's forty-five out of its drawer, and joked about who'd kill who. I saw he was drunk.

He was sitting at the dining table, and I was standing near the window, telling him not to point that thing in my direction, and he was telling how Pop never keeps it loaded.

Just then Nicky's cat jumped up on the window ledge outside and cried to me. I turned to look, and moved one step toward the window, and as I did the gun went off and blew a hole half the size of my head in the wall where I'd been.

I had the eerie sensation that I'd felt the bullet go by, and my ear tickled, too much to be real, but knowing that didn't make it stop.

I cried, but Michael cried harder. That scared me worse than the shot, because Michael crying was like god saying I give up, I don't know what comes next.

He kept saying, "Things just happen, Francie. How do you stop them? I don't know how to stop them. They just happen."

"What happened, Michael? Pop would never tell me what happened to Nicky."

I had to wait while Michael stopped crying, but then he told me that a man outside a bar stabbed Nicky for something he thought he did. It was an ugly death, he said, and that's why Pop didn't want me to know.

"Ugly how?" I said. "Where did the man stab him?"

"Low belly."

It didn't sound ugly. I pictured a knife being stuck in Nicky's lower belly and that being the end of it.

"He didn't exactly stab him," Michael explained. "He cut him. Hip to hip. Opened him up. When that happens, it's hard to keep everything inside that's meant to be inside."

I wished to god then that I hadn't asked.

By this time I was shaking pretty bad and Michael helped me upstairs and I lay down on my bed.

I woke up a few hours later. It was dark, and Pop still wasn't home. Michael was in a chair in the corner, staring at me. His unshaven face twitched, and he sat with his knees apart and his feet together, jiggling one leg.

"Do you have to stare at me like that?" I said.

He got up and walked to the window. The moon was hanging almost full over the trees, and I watched his back.

"Goodnight, moon," he said. "Goodnight, room. Goodnight man in the moon. Remember when Mom used to read us that book? There was a mouse on every page. You could never find it—I always had to show you where it was."

"You had a few years on me," I said. "For a long time I thought all kids brought books to their mother's bed for their bedtime stories. I didn't know mothers made house calls."

"She couldn't help it if she was sick."

I felt close to Michael, and I wanted to share something with him. Last time I'd noticed loving him that much was when I watched him take a whipping.

"Did you read that story Nicky wrote? About Mom? Well, most of it wasn't about Mom, but that was the central point."

He turned back from the window and his face looked strained in the moonlight. "The one about Peppy the talking dog? Nicky didn't write that. I did."

I wanted to argue that I'd seen Nicky's name on it, but I didn't, because Nicky never could have written that—it wasn't in him to do it. I wondered why I hadn't known all along.

Michael came over to my bed and lay down. "Move over," he said. He was shaking so hard that the bed shook with him.

When I woke up again, he was in the chair in the corner, his face red and stained, his eyes puffy like he'd been crying for weeks. He said, "I was in town when Nicky died."

"I know." I didn't know I knew until I said it.

"You knew that? Does Pop know?"

I sat up and shrugged. "Pop would think the worst about you anyway. He thinks earthquakes and floods are your fault."

Michael wiped his nose on his sleeve. "If I tell you this do you promise to forgive me?"

I liked that my forgiveness meant something to him, so I nodded, even though I really needed to hear the story to know. And then, just like that, I knew. And I didn't need to hear the story at all.

"That man thought Nicky was you."

He looked up at me, quick and shy, then dropped his gaze to the carpet and jiggled his leg some more.

"Do you forgive me?"

"I don't think that would help, Michael. I think you gotta get Nicky to forgive you."

"Nicky's dead, stupid. It's a little late for that."

I felt awed by my responsibility. "You're going to have to pray to him." I don't know where the words came from. I never prayed.

"I don't believe in god," he said. "I'm not praying."

"I didn't say pray to god. Pray to Nicky. To forgive you. I mean it, Michael. This is important."

Michael got down on his knees beside my bed. "I don't know how to do this. Nicky's not god."

"But he's in heaven. So just say, 'Our brother. Our brother, who art in heaven.'"

"This is stupid," he said. He stamped out of my room, slamming the door behind him.

Pop got home after midnight. Michael was long gone.

He took one look at the hole in the wall and said, "Michael is never to come in this house again, understand?"

I said I did.

And the sad part was, I really did.

LOST CAUSES

*M*y father was a married man. Well, I guess that sounds weird to say. Like, whose isn't? But when Marcia says that—Marcia, that's my mother—what she means is, *already*. Like, he already was when she met him. Not to her.

She made this deal that she'd keep her mouth shut and he'd send support, just nice and quiet, and nobody's life would get all disrupted, which I pretty much take to mean, not his. In sixteen years, Marcia says, he's sent a total of twelve hundred dollars.

Blow the fucking whistle on him, I said. She won't. I know she won't. He knows she won't. It bugs me, that he relies on her good nature like that. His life is still all together because she's terminally polite.

Sometimes I think I could be vindictive for her.

I met him once. He treated me like a virus.

But Stanley. Stanley slipped through my radar. I thought he was a Good Guy. Turns out Marcia sort of half-assed knew better, but she kept it to herself, like if nobody else knows it, it doesn't count. Like when she went back to smoking last year, hanging out the bathroom window, blowing smoke into twenty-degree nights, calling herself a nonsmoker for the first four months, because up until then nobody saw her at it. So far as she knew.

I think this is a bad comment about Marcia's self-esteem, that she doesn't even count herself a valid witness. Okay, I borrowed most of that from my County Mental Health Counselor. We were talking about me at the time.

Stanley took me to a Dodgers game once, when I was fourteen. That is how long this guy has been around. I mean, he is a real recordbreaker in Marcia's life, that Stanley. I had that typical girl's attitude about baseball, but parts of it were pretty okay. It was a night game, and I mostly remember this high pop fly, the way it arced up right across the moon. Stanley bought me two hot dogs and let me drink half his beer.

I kind of always knew he was attracted to me, but that didn't make him a bad guy. Not necessarily.

First of all, old guys are just like that. It's like a switch that's around on their back, where somebody else turns it on and they can't do a damn thing about it. It's like something with chemicals. I'm not even sure it's about me. And also, it's not like he ever tried to make anything happen with that. If I maybe had tried at that point, I think the chemicals and the switch thing, it would have been too much for him. He probably would have tumbled real nice and easy. I thought about it from time to time but that's all. It's hard not to think about something that would be so easy, so completely predictable, like dropping a bowling ball out a window. They say no guarantees in this life but I say it'll fall.

He had a lot of hair on his chest, I know, even though at that point I had only seen the way it pooched out the collar of his shirt, and it was starting to go gray. The skin was loose at his neck and I guess I would have been scared to see more than that. At the time. He had a silver chain disappearing down into his shirt. I can't remember if I ever wondered what was at the end of it.

Once I asked Marcia why she never went over to his house. She said it was something she didn't care to discuss. I figured that meant if she discussed it, then it might be real.

Score one for me.

The night Stanley lost his good-guy status, I had been out losing my virginity. Sixteen is old for that. The girls at school said I must either be gay or hopeless—all except Kara Franklin, who I think is my friend, at least somewhat. She said if I was gay I would have lost it with a girl by now, so I must be hopeless. She actually said this in sort of a nice way. It's hard to explain.

I think it was more that I was a little overweight, not enough to be a total disaster, but enough that it felt weird to think about taking my clothes off with a guy, and it must have felt weird for them to want me to. It's one thing to aim to lose your virginity, quite another to find a guy who wants it, and is willing to admit that.

I even thought about Stanley, but I wasn't sure a guy that old would count. I figured it had to be a guy from our school, a name to drop, so everyone would know this was someone real. Besides, Marcia was still using Stanley, at the time.

So it ended up being Mickey Spirelli.

Mickey took me along when he went babysitting, at his friends the Willises, who are grownups. But I think they are actually his friends, even so. They had two kids, both asleep, which was good, and a car you could hear all the way down to the freeway. It whistled. Mickey said you could see the road right through a hole in the floorboard of that car, which they called Alexander. I said, *Oh, really?* But it turned out I was supposed to ask why. *Okay, why?* I said. Because it's *Goodenov* for them. Get it? It was the Willis's joke, not Mickey's. I mean, he didn't think it up. I think they'd been telling that one for years.

We played this board game with a foreign name, Mille Bournes, for a while, even though we knew what we had come here for. I had even shaved my legs and under my arms—that's how much I knew. It felt weird at first, so we played this game. Rhoda, the Willis's basset hound, sat under the table scratching. There were fleas all over that house, not just on the dog. They kept jars of water on the tables, to drop the fleas into when you picked them off your legs.

After a while we went to bed. The lights were all off in the bedroom, so it didn't feel bad to get undressed. Mickey got nervous. We lay under the covers naked for awhile, and he told me a true story, which was a brave thing to do. Considering the story. He said once he was at a party, and some guys threw him into a room with a girl. He didn't know this girl. I guess this girl would do just about anybody. Not that Mickey was so bad, just that she didn't exactly need to know you. He got kind of scared and couldn't do it.

I forgot to mention that Mickey was a virgin, but he was younger than me, only fifteen, which maybe helps a little. But I guess not much.

I got a feeling he was telling me the story for a reason, and that we were both still going to be virgins for a while. He tried pretending I wasn't there for a minute, but that didn't help nearly enough.

After a while I felt like I ought to let him off the hook. I said *let's go back in the kitchen and play that foreign game some more and maybe we'll try this again later. If you want.*

We played the game until we'd set about six more fleas floating around in the jar, and then he told me I had said exactly the right thing. I was surprised. I thought, *I'll have to remember that. Let them off the hook.*

We went back to bed, and pretty much did it. It kind of hurt and kind of felt good at the same time. He finished. I'm not sure what I did. I wasn't sure if I was supposed to do anything. I was glad we were both cherry, because if there was something to know, maybe he wouldn't know it either.

The kids never woke up, and we got dressed in plenty of time before the Willises got home, because we could hear Alexander whistle in.

I'm not sure why I mention all of that, or if it's important. It was to me, though.

When I got home, I came into the house through my bedroom window. I'm not sure why. Or I'm just not sure how to expain why. It was like something had changed. If I had to talk to Marcia, and if she said, *How was your date?* and I had to make something up, or tell the truth, either one, it might change back on me. Actually, that's one good thing about losing your virginity: never having to worry that you'll get it back unexpectedly. But it felt like something I had to hold onto, at least for the time being. So everything wouldn't go ordinary on me again.

It was about midnight, and I heard her talking to Stanley in the living room. Low voices, I couldn't make out the words. Something felt wrong about it. I opened the bedroom door, nice and quiet.

She was sitting on his lap on the couch, crying. He was stroking her hair with one hand, wiping tears off her face with the other, like it would kill him to leave them there. There was something real intense about the way he leaned into her, and kept his face close.

He kept saying, "I'm sorry. I'm sorry. I'm sorry."

I wanted to say, *What did you do to her, you son of a bitch?*

I know, I said he was a nice guy, but right at that moment I knew I'd been wrong. Whatever he was sorry about, he damn well ought to be. That much was real clear.

Marcia blew her nose on a paper towel, and talked too loud. "Remember that time, about a month after I met you, and I told you I had that dream where I met your ex-wife, and I asked her how long you'd been divorced, and she said, 'Oh, Stanley and I are not divorced'?" Stanley was nodding, real hard. He not only remembered, I think he might have wished he didn't have to remember again now. "That's how long I've known," she said, with that hush to her voice she should have had all along. "In here."

I knew the spot she pointed to. It hurts in there.

"Known what?" I asked.

Stanley stood up and Marcia fell back onto the couch, and tried to wipe her eyes with the paper towel. All she got for her trouble was mascara wreckage.

"How long have you been home?" I forget which one of them said that.

Marcia said, "How was your date, honey?" like what was happening to her could turn invisible.

Then I remembered how easy my date would be to ruin, after the fact. So I went back in my bedroom, to hold on a little bit longer.

Marcia called in sick to work for six days. She had a way of taking things hard, which I was always afraid I might inherit. She had to call her doctor and tell him she had the flu. He said drink lots of water, and call him for antibiotics if it got worse. Which it didn't, of course, because it didn't exist. She did it because, later, when it was time to go back to work, his nurse would write one of those nice little notes. "Marcia consulted our office regarding her flu." More than three days and they wouldn't let her back to work without it.

Marcia had this falling apart bit down to a science.

"What a perfect time to leave the whole world behind and fly away to Mexico," she said. Then she walked down to the corner liquor store and bought a giant economy-size bottle of Cuervo Gold and that was her Mexican vacation. She made it last four days.

"How could you not know he was married, Marcia?" I just said that out of nowhere one morning.

It was the fourth day. I'd been smart enough not to bring it up so far. All of a sudden I got stupid. I was skipping school that day, in fact I'd skipped three of those four days and she'd been too far south of the border to notice.

"It's a complicated situation, Tracy." She was wearing her sunglasses at the breakfast table again. Not a good sign. She kept playing that Foreigner song over and over, about yesterday being gone, pushing the repeat button on the CD player before we could move on to something we hadn't already heard all night.

"It seems pretty simple to me. You couldn't go to his house. Didn't you ask why?"

"Of course I did. Don't patronize me, kiddo. Remember who the adult is here."

"What did he say?"

"He said his ex-wife was being a problem. It was just a scratchy situation. She'd had kind of a breakdown. And lost her job, and he'd let her move back in. Just for a little while. He asked me to be patient."

"For two years?"

"When you love a man you want to trust him."

I'd never thought about the fact that she might love Stanley. Then I realized I didn't want to think about it now. But I had to ask the final question.

"How'd you find out?"

"His wife told me. I met her by accident." I knew all about Marcia's accidents. "She's a successful therapist. Makes good money. Which is a little different from what he said. She does marriage counseling. I asked if that got awkward, a divorced marriage counselor. She just kind of looked at me . . ." Her voice trailed off. Tears rolled out from under her sunglasses.

"What a bastard," I said. I headed for my room so I didn't have to watch any more of this.

Just before I closed the door, I heard her say, "I wish it was all black and white like that, Trace. Good guys and bad guys."

"It is," I said. And shut the door.

I called up Mickey and asked him to skip with me. First he said he might flunk geometry if he did, but those guy hormones always tip the scales. He came over, and by that time Marcia was asleep, because she'd doubled up on her Xanax and killed her Mexican Vacation In A Bottle.

I took a shower with Mickey, which was, like, the most I'd ever let him see me naked. Broad daylight and all.

I said I hated my body—it was too fat. He said it was beautiful. And, I mean, he was looking right at it. I figured that was a lie, but I liked him for it anyway.

Then all of a sudden I started wondering. Like, how do you know if something's a lie or it isn't? I wondered if there was anything about Mickey I should know that would make me say later, "If I had only known." Before, I'm not sure I would have had that thought. I mean, you take your clothes off with somebody. You'd think you'd know all about them, right? You think somebody is all exposed. But then, once you start to doubt that—I mean, how do you know?

I wondered how Marcia was ever going to trust anybody again, only somehow I knew she would, because she just would. That was just her. I'd seen it before, I knew I was about to see it again.

I didn't end up doing anything with Mickey that day. I never really said why, or even exactly knew myself, but it felt weird. Once you do it the first time, it's kind of a given. I think.

A week went by. Marcia went back to work, and Mickey didn't call me. And I didn't call him. I decided it was just like him to dump me for holding out that one time. I decided that was one of those things I wished I had known about him.

You never really know about somebody.

Another week or two crawled by, and everything stayed quiet, the kind of quiet I always wish for. Then when I get it, it's never what I had in mind.

I'd been hanging out at The Bean, on the patio, with six or seven guys and a girl, playing handball until the owner threatened to call the cops. This guy I didn't even know was buying me cappuccinos at two bucks a pop.

When everybody ran out of money we got thrown out. Some of the guys were going to a party, but I decided to cut loose of Mr. Cappuccino before he got it in his head I owed him something.

I ended up at home earlier than expected.

There's Marcia, on the couch, going at it in the dark with some guy. Not naked or anything, but you could tell they'd get there soon enough. Total unstoppable passion. I thought, All *right*, Marcia. Just get right back up on the horse. I was pretty sure I didn't stand to inherit that side of her.

They looked up as I tried to slip by.

"Don't mind me," I said. They both jumped, like they'd been caught robbing the store. "Stanley?" I said. "You're with fucking Stanley? What did I miss?"

Stanley got up and tucked his shirt in, flustered, making noises about leaving.

"No," Marcia said. "Don't go, Stan. Wait for me in the bedroom."

He did just like he was told. Never looked me in the eye, either. I figured that said a lot.

Marcia patted the couch beside her leg but I didn't want to sit with her just then.

"Boy, that'll teach him to lie to you," I said.

"Don't, Trace." The way her voice was, I decided not to say anything else. After a big, bad silence, she said, "There's no way you could possibly understand."

But I could see how things were changing for her, right there, in front of me, and now all of a sudden she couldn't possibly understand, either. She'd been caught doing this thing, and now she had to see it through my eyes. I watched the truth shift around inside her. She looked over her shoulder at the bedroom door, and I knew she wouldn't go in.

After a while she picked up her car keys and headed out the front door.

I was way too wired up on caffeine to sleep. I sat on the couch and channel-surfed until I found that old black-and-white movie *Invaders From Mars*. I stopped there and watched it, tapping one of my feet on the coffee table. I wondered what exactly Marcia had consumed. I was edgy about her being on the road in one of her "what does my life really add up to?" crises.

I half-expected Stanley to show a little class and make himself scarce through the bedroom window. Instead he came out and sat on the couch beside me, combing his hair halfway back into line with his fingers. He stared at the screen like it was fascinating, just what he would have picked out to watch himself.

After a while he said, "Where'd she go?"

"Hell if I know."

He stared at the screen a while longer. "She knows I didn't want to hurt her. I—"

I held a hand up to stop him, and he stopped. We just sat there staring at TV for almost an hour. I kept glancing over at the side of his face, which was a mistake, because it reminded me that I had always liked him. I couldn't seem to frame him with all this new information. Maybe that was Marcia's problem, kind of a time-lag thing. She shifts gears real slow. I started wishing he would go away so I could hate him. I'd been doing just fine with that while he wasn't around.

The phone rang, and we both jumped. I got up to answer it. It was Marcia. *Where the hell are you?* I said. *Don't you think I worry about you? Do you have any idea how late it is?*

She said she was in Seal Beach, and that she needed to drive around some more. She asked if he was still there. *Get rid of him,* she said. *I'll be home in an hour or two.*

Sad as it is to say, I kind of understood how she had to go all the way to Seal Beach before she could get strong about him again. But I was right there with him. I didn't have that luxury of distance.

I walked back over and sat down on his lap. That whole hour we'd been sitting together I'd known I was about to do something, even halfway known why, but I was careful not to think it out in words.

I could see his Adam's apple jump when he swallowed.

"What are you doing, Trace?" he asked.

He'd never called me Trace before. Other people had, but it sounded different when he said it, like it occurred to me for the first time that a *trace* is something that's hardly there at all.

"I'm doing this," I said, and I kissed him.

But it was only me kissing him for a second, then the whole thing seemed to flip on me. His tongue was in my mouth, and I could feel him kind of gearing up for it, real fast. Surprised, but right there to meet it. It felt scary, like too much power, like the first time I shifted Marcia's car into drive and hit the gas.

He carried me into the bedroom. Marcia's bedroom.

On the way in he said, "Are you sure this is what you want?"

I don't remember what I said, only that I could have stopped everything right there, but I didn't. I was glad he asked, though, because the whole thing had gotten way beyond me, and something about being physically carried like that, well, I was just glad to be reminded that my consent still factored in there somewhere.

And then, the funny thing was, he let me be on top. I'm not sure why. I just remember leaning my hands on his chest, trying to remember what my original plan was. Like, why I thought this would tell me what I wanted to know.

I thought since he was older, and a tall guy, that he'd be real big, painfully so, and it would really tear me up, but he was about the same size as Mickey—which wasn't saying much— and shaped kind of funny. I remember thinking Marcia never told me that. I mean, of course she didn't; why should she? But I guess I mean it felt weird that now we both knew. I don't think I ever intended to have that much in common with Marcia, but I didn't think of that in time.

Something about that, the smallness and strange shape of him, and the way his stomach was soft, it felt like some deep weakness in him. Like a tender spot. It felt amazing that it was even something he would let me see. It was like a soft, underbelly, literally, that I knew and he knew I could use to hurt him if I wanted. Just by noticing. And part of me did want to hurt him. Just a few minutes ago I'd been wanting that.

It seemed like it was over fast, the kind of fast that makes you wonder what the whole thing's supposed to be for.

I stayed there on him a while, feeling so grown up it was scary. The skin on his shoulders and around his collarbone was translucent. I remember thinking, *What protects you?*

I picked up the silver chain. His eyelids had drifted half-closed. The chain seemed to have a medallion weighing it down, but it had slid around under his shoulder. I gently worked it loose. His eyes opened.

He said, "I'm not sure why you wanted to do that, but I can't say I'm sorry."

But I remembered him saying it to Marcia, over and over. *I'm sorry. I'm sorry. I'm sorry.*

"What is this?" I said. I meant the medallion.

"Saint Jude."

"What does he take care of?"

"Lost causes."

"I never heard of a Jude medal. Only Christopher."

"They have medals for all the saints."

"Are you Catholic?"

"No."

"I didn't think so." I stayed on him while we talked about this, because it felt more and more like the driver's seat. "So, maybe you're not good or bad," I said. "Maybe you're just a lost cause."

He looked up at me, kind of curious, and it struck me again how he'd left himself open, like he trusted the way I'd use all this new leverage. Maybe he shouldn't have.

He said, "Is that what you're after? Trying to figure out if I'm good or bad?"

"Maybe."

Or whether I was good or bad. Because maybe if I could do something bad, which this clearly was, then maybe I could understand why he could. Or maybe I'd understand why Marcia could sleep with him, even after he'd hurt her like that, if I could do it, too. Or maybe I wanted to prove he was really bad, all bad, pond scum through and through, the kind of guy who would sleep with his girlfriend's teenage daughter. But now, with his soft stomach and that skin I could almost see through, that plan felt too much like police entrapment. Anybody will tell you that's not really fair.

"So what did you decide?" he said.

"I'm confused now."

"Then you're a lot closer to the truth," he said, and kind of moved me off him.

"What's the truth?" I asked, maybe a little desperate, because I thought he might get away without telling me, and then the whole thing would be for nothing.

He said, "The truth is confusing," then he put on his pants.

I didn't see him after that, and far as I know, she didn't either. I'm still not sure if he was good or bad, or somewhere in between like Marcia. Like me. But I'm convinced now that he was right in what he said about the truth. So that's something.

EARTHQUAKE WEATHER

*I*t's seven-thirty in the morning and Angie sits in her Jeep. Before she starts the engine she reaches out to the dash, where dust has settled thick overnight, and with the tip of her finger, writes *Happy Independence Day*.

Then, underneath, she writes Joe's name, stares at it a minute, and fires up the Jeep.

It is not the Fourth of July.

In fact, it's all of September 10, but here in Benton it's hot. Earthquake weather, they call it in LA, where she's glad she's not. Heavy and muggy. Even in this early morning it hangs beneath the air, not heat exactly, but the promise or threat of it.

Angie cranks down the window and heads for the highway.

She passes an old tractor and makes a mental note. *See if there's a parts store in town, and does it stock diesel?* If so, she can fix it. Angie can fix anything. She's worked on cars and ranch equipment since she was a young girl, and if it ran once she can make it run again.

Three years of therapy taught her she did this to impress her father. If it *had* impressed him she might have understood her motive sooner.

The town of Benton is three blocks of Main Street, with a feed store, but no parts store, a couple of gas stations, a market, a diner she's been advised to avoid, and a bakery.

The bakery is the social heart of town, an old tumbledown building on the corner of Main and Spruce. Converted from a gas station and drive-through bait store, it remains close to its roots in the way it greets the eye.

Stepping inside, Angie smells deep fat and donut glaze.

Three small tables make up the sitting area, on a floor plagued by waxy buildup over dirt.

The coffee is strong, even for her. She buys a cinnamon twist to go with it. It's warm and drips glaze on her plate.

A high school girl snaps gum behind the counter. Angie meets one other local. He looks up from his paper, says, "Morning." Asks if she's just passing through.

"Not anymore," she says.

He's a tall man with grayish-white hair, fifty or more, but he looks good. The years have left ruts in his face but he knows how to wear them. He seems to fit well in his clothes, in his skin. Angie pictures Natalie growing up a local, with none of the wild-eyed corruption of the city. Becoming a tall, strong young woman with the look of this man, a knowing stillness, like the steady eye of a good ranch horse.

His name is Ben. Angie tells him as little as possible. Her anonymity is gone, the city stripped away like a blanket, and she sees herself under a magnifying glass, feeling known.

"I bought the ranch over on Old Creek Road," she says.

"All by yourself?"

"Well, no. My husband will be joining me in a day or two." *He should have been here yesterday.*

"And my daughter will be here today. She's been staying with my mother during the move." *During the separation.*

He welcomes her, and his eyes drop back to his paper. He wears a wedding ring. She wonders why she thought to look.

As she glances around for a clock, Angie sees the girl behind the counter staring, blowing bubbles with her gum. She wonders if this girl heard the parts she didn't say.

It's nine o'clock, and Angie gazes through the post office window. A heavy woman in no hurry unlocks the door.

On the wall is a bank of private boxes, maybe forty. Angie's is number twenty-three, and there is a letter in it. A first letter. Her hands shake as she works the combination, which makes her angry.

She recognizes Joe's writing, and wonders if this is what she wanted or what she didn't want, but she won't know until she opens it, which she doesn't want to do.

She stares at the envelope until she realizes that an old couple is eyeing her. Angie smiles, and in an imitation of normality, opens the letter.

It's short. It says, "Angie. I hope you will understand what I'm about to say." Angie knows she won't.

> *I know you thought this move would fix everything, and up until yesterday I wanted to agree. Today everything is different, because we just found out that Meg is pregnant. It was magnanimous of you to suggest that you'll forgive everything if I give her up, but now I can't do that.*
> *Tell Nattie I love her and we'll work out a visitation.*
> *Maybe we'll talk when you've had time to adjust.*

"Maybe not," Angie says out loud, crumpling the letter into a ball. She launches it toward the waste bin in the corner, misses by a mile. It skitters across the floor and stays there.

The old couple turns to look again.

It's the hottest part of the following afternoon and Angie has chosen this time to cut mustard weed. She'd hoped to get the tractor going and mow the damn stuff, but instead is chopping it with a machete. There are fifteen or twenty acres of it, and she knows only a fool would try to take it out by hand.

Thoughts come up but she swallows them again, like bile rising in her throat. Her back muscles knot, but if she stops she won't know what to do, so she doesn't stop.

Finally it's time to pick up Natalie from her new kindergarten, and Angie is relieved. She can stop now, because something else requires her.

"I have a surprise for you," she says when Nattie climbs into the Jeep.

"My pony's here!" Nattie is always one step ahead. They

were delivered today, Nattie's Shetland and Angie's new horse. "Mom," she asks, "when's Daddy coming?"

Angie feels her daughter's stare. While she's not answering her head spins.

"He's not, honey."

Nattie says, "Oh."

Crossing the bridge to their new property, Nattie speaks up again. "Mommy. Are you mad at him?"

Angie thinks it over, then says, "No. He did something I don't like, but I'm not mad."

Nattie says, "Oh."

It's after four. The light is on a good slant, but it's still hot. Dust settles in Angie's nose and throat as she and Nattie ride the ridge by the south fence line.

Nattie's pony is a good one, a fuzzy little Shetland, mottled tan with a thick white mane and tail. Jet, Angie's new mustang, is jumpy. Or maybe it's Angie. She senses that they don't like each other yet, and together they ride a safe arc around their mistrust.

A tall outcropping of rocks stands on the right, a sharp drop-off to the left. As they come around the rock hill, they see cattle grazing across the fence on the neighboring ranch.

Jet sees them, spooks straight up. When he lands, one back hoof slips off the edge of the trail. Angie kicks him forward but he rears and spins, and now his whole back end is over. He scrambles for footing and she curses and kicks, each movement an electric shock to the muscles of her over-worked back.

Perfect ranch horse, they told me. Except he's never seen a cow before. Great.

Nattie's pony stands spraddle-legged and watches with mild curiosity as Jet looses a shower of rocks and slips further. Angie uses a length of rein to smack him hard on the rump.

As if in slow motion, before he can react, Angie knows she doesn't want to play. She's not emotionally up to this moment, and she wants out. It feels like the flu, a big gaping hole where her energy and spirit should be.

Get me out of this, she thinks, but doesn't know who she's addressing.

Jet reacts with a terrified surge of forward motion. In one valiant jump he is back on the trail, sides heaving.

Angie slides down, walks the mile back to the barn, Nattie on her pony following faithfully behind.

In the morning, she thinks, *I can always take him back.*

Nattie unsaddles her own pony.

The light is nearly gone. The last rays glare through the periphery of Angie's unblinking eyes. She stares at Jet, who stares back. He has a heavy forelock and a long, straight black face, and his eyes blame her for everything.

She picks up his hooves to check them. She holds a back foot, and he pulls it away in a half-hearted kick, which misses.

Angie snaps, grabs the bridle off the hitching post, lights into him, waling his rump relentlessly.

His neck strains as he pulls against the rope in panic. A cloud of dust from his thrashing hooves obscures his black barrel.

Lost in the relief of rage, Angie forgets to worry for the whereabouts of her daughter.

Then, from the corner of her eye, she sees Nattie behind one stout pole of the hitching post, holding it tightly with both arms.

Weak rays halo her thin blond hair. She looks like her father.

Angie freezes, seeing herself through her daughter's eyes. Jet calms to a nervous dance, neck arched, muscles taut and prepared.

"Mommy," she says, "are you mad at Jet?"

With conviction, Angie says, "Yes I am."

"Did he do something you didn't like?"

"Yes, honey. A couple things."

"Worse than what Dad did?"

Angie drops the bridle, and her sigh deflates her.

"Go in the house and wash up for dinner, honey. I'll put your pony away."

When she is out of sight Angie buries her face against Jet's taut black neck, the closest Angie will come to an apology.

When she draws back again she sees him watching her with one wild, white-rimmed eye.

In the small hours of morning, Angie wakes.

She thinks of Joe, at home, in bed. With Meg.

Meg of the cold war, the unspoken struggle.

Meg who sneered behind her Ray-Bans when Angie announced plans for another baby after the reconciliation. Sneered because she knew so much that Angie didn't.

Angie tries to think of something else. Nattie's pony. Nattie named her Minnie. Nattie would outgrow Minnie in a few years, but she would stay on as a pet.

When I picked her out, I thought she'd be a hand-me-down for a second child.

Now Angie feels there are no safe thoughts.

She pulls on jeans and yesterday's shirt, which she doesn't bother to button or tuck in. Outside, the breeze is cool, but barely. Angie looks at the moon and thinks of animals that howl in their lonely need. She throws back her head but no sound escapes.

Angie drops Nattie at school early and drives to the bakery.

She steps through the door, wonders if she'll see Ben.

She doesn't know what she wants from him, only that she wants something, and that she doesn't have it.

Ben arrives at quarter past seven and says, "Morning."

Angie knows now that she looks to him because he is that human imitation of the immovable force. Steady, like the ground—or at least the ground in Benton.

One of many reasons Angie left LA is because the ground should never move. This is the ultimate betrayal.

Angie follows him with her eyes, pondering her need.

Her restlessness has become a daily struggle. She moves from place to place, knowing when she arrives that she is in the wrong location.

Ben looks up from his paper and smiles, shy and flattered, and Angie looks away.

The gum-snapping counter girl is watching her, and Angie picks up a section of newspaper and pretends to read.

Don't let the poison touch him. Not Ben.

In time Ben moves on to Ben's day, and Angie is rooted to her chair, unwilling to face the emptiness she is sure waits just outside the bakery door.

A younger man comes in, and Angie recognizes him as the mechanic from the Texaco station.

Her first impression of him was unflattering: *Thinks he's James Dean.*

Now it doesn't seem to matter what he thinks.

He stands at the counter, faced away, a narrow triangle of sweat staining the back of his shirt. His short sleeves are rolled and his biceps muscled. His butt is round and full and his jeans are torn in several places.

He turns back, sipping his coffee, sits by the window. He seems aware of Angie's stare.

Several strands of hair fall across his forehead. An embroidered patch on his shirt says "Curtis." He wears a thin gold band on his left ring finger.

Angie thinks of asking if he does diesel mechanics. *I do diesel,* she could have said. But she can find no patience for small talk.

She stands and walks to his table. Sits down, uninvited. Opens the window. It's not even eight o'clock, but hot.

Indian Summer. Earthquake weather.

She sits sideways, her back against the window. Stretches out her long legs, liking the look of jeans over boots, breaking and bunching. Runs her hands through her short black hair, finger-combing it back, a pantomime for the heat.

"So, Curtis," she says, though they have never spoken before. "Any *single* men in this town?"

Angie catches the flash of his white teeth—she knows she is getting closer; but to what?

"Not so's you'd notice," Curtis says.

It is ten at night and Curtis sits in the dirt beside Angie, opens a pint of Southern Comfort. She did not invite him, but she was not surprised when he arrived.

He passes it to Angie, who takes a deep swallow, watching the stars through the thin veil of scrub oaks.

More stars in Benton than in LA. More stars in Benton than anywhere.

Curtis sounds soft and distant now, telling his sad story. How he's been married over a year, how his wife has had sex with him three times. How cold she gets if he tries to talk about it.

Angie is glad Curtis is here, and she doesn't care what propelled him, but she allows him to talk.

Then she listens to crickets and silence, her thoughts moving farther and farther away.

She thinks of telling him of her eleven months of separation and struggle with Joe, the raw nerves it left behind. She tells him only to pass the bottle. She is single and her willingness requires no explanation.

For the first time in several days, her mind is easy.

Curtis suggests they wander up over the rise. Angie says she wants to stay close to the house, to her sleeping child. They end up in a deep gully, close enough to hear Nattie call.

Nattie doesn't call.

Curtis's hands fumble for her shirt buttons. The light of a soft moon washes over them, glints across the gold of his ring.

It is three AM. Angie is alone with a disturbing dream.

She is five, just Nattie's age. She is in her father's house. Her mother is away in the hospital. She tiptoes into her father's room, climbs into bed for comfort. In the dark she feels the presence of a stranger.

The strange woman sits up, more frightened of Angie than Angie is frightened of her. Her father grabs her by one arm and carries her back to her room. She lies in bed shaking. Her shoulder hurts, but she doesn't cry.

Awake now, Angie plays the dream over. She hasn't thought about it since it happened, but she knows it's not just a dream.

Sitting in the second-floor window, Angie looks out over the front porch. In her father's ranch house, her room had a similar view.

She remembers the night her mother came home with the drunken cowboy, his truck weaving and lurching up the road. The way he half walked, half chased her mother to the front door. Saying, "Come 'ere, girl," over and over again. Her shrill laughter as she shushed him.

She remembers the way her mother grabbed and patted the crotch of his jeans before launching him, staggering, back to his truck.

When she is done remembering, she takes the only available action, the one she took that night when she was ten. She goes back to bed and tries to sleep.

It is October 16th and still hot.

Angie sees Curtis on Main Street. She has not seen him for two weeks. He came by every night for twelve nights, then the visits stopped.

Angie's addiction to the presence of his body is shaming in its proportions. She feels like a junkie sweating it out.

Seeing him is a jolt.

He is walking with his wife, who is seven or eight months pregnant. Angie walks the other way.

He catches up with her around the corner, takes her by the arm. "I know what you're thinking," he says, "but it was one of those three times I told you about."

Angie takes her arm back and walks to her Jeep.

Driving down Main Street, she sees Ben's truck and parks around the corner from it.

In the market, she buys a card with horses on the outside, blank inside. Back at the Jeep, Angie writes inside.

"You have an admirer. I'm not trying to start anything. I just want you to know."

She seals it and places it on the windshield of Ben's truck.

As she is driving away, Angie thinks he might be in town with his wife, or children. She feels the descent of responsibility for the act.

She parks across the street and waits until she sees Ben walk to his truck, alone. He waves to Angie and she smiles and pulls away.

Now he knows—which she hadn't planned—but she decides that's okay.

It is a Friday morning, and Jet is being loaded into a two-horse trailer. Angie is relieved to see him go.

She is trading him to a young man for fence repair. He has not been ridden since that first day.

Inside, Angie reads the classifieds, circles several ads.

She starts at the beginning of the column. Appaloosa mare. Sixteen two hands but gentle enough for a child.

She phones the number, and a gracious woman answers. Her ranch is only six miles away. The woman gives clear directions.

She greets Angie and leads her to a stall in the back of the barn. Her hair is gray with traces of blond, her smile soft and courteous.

"I have to go into town," she says, "but my husband is coming in right now to show you the mare."

She says they are only selling her because their youngest daughter moved away to college.

She drives off and Angie paces the barn aisle alone.

She hears hoofbeats, and looks up to see Ben ride into the barn on a compact buckskin. He dismounts, his face flushed and shy. He shakes Angie's hand as though they had never met, halters the mare and leads her out into the light.

She is a big, solid leopard Appy, white with black spots, a trimmed mane. She seems docile and her eyes are calm.

Ben takes his saddle off the buckskin, a broad saddle with a suede seat. He saddles the mare, then mounts her without a bridle, controlling her only with the halter rope.

"She neck reins," he says.

Angie says nothing. It is all she can do to feel her boot soles on the ground, and not to look Ben in the eye.

"She's big enough you can even ride her double. You and your husband could ride together."

He reaches a hooked arm down, slips his left foot out of the stirrup. Angie takes his arm and swings up behind him. Squeezed into the back of the big saddle, her thighs crush against him.

Ben reins the mare around and heads out along a tree-lined trail between two pastures.

They ride in silence for a time, then Ben nudges the mare to a gentle, rolling lope, and Angie puts an arm around his waist, though she is in no danger of falling.

In time she rides with her other hand on his thigh, the way she would ride behind Joe on his motorcycle. The familiarity of the gesture seems unnoticed, as though planned.

Ben slows the horse to a walk as they head up the hill.

"You made my day with that," he says; Angie wishes he hadn't.

"I wasn't trying to start with you."

"I believe you mentioned that."

Ben stops the horse, kicks out of the stirrups, and swings a leg over her neck, dropping to the ground.

"Go on, take her out," he says. "I'll be right here."

Angie takes the mare over hills, into gullies, thinks she can see the ocean, feels sweat creep down the back of her collar.

The mare is push-button trained; nothing unnerves her. Angie never wants to bring her back because she hasn't decided what to say to Ben.

Ben is a stranger.

It doesn't seem fair to use him as the standard of measure. She has no reason to cast him as the solid earth. Knowing this does not change her view of him.

She takes the mare in a circle without knowing it, sees Ben in the distance, rides to him.

He is at her waist level, she looks down into his face.

"What if I *had* tried to start something, then what?"

His face is open, unafraid. He says, "Is this a trick question? What do you want me to say?"

Angie thinks about this, maybe too long. "I want you to say you wouldn't have budged."

"You do? Why?"

"I want to think you would have been faithful to your wife."

"Why?"

"Somebody has to be."

The mare shifts underneath Angie, rubs her muzzle on the inside of a front leg.

Ben's face clouds. "Of course I want to be faithful to my wife," he says. "But I'm just a man."

"Don't say that."

The earth should never move. It's the ultimate betrayal.

"Is that all you want from me? You just want me to say I won't sleep with you?"

"No," Angie says, "I want this mare, too."

Far down the hill, Ben's wife returns, her car pursued by clouds of dust, and nothing of the sort is ever mentioned again.

Within a month the weather turns nippy.

Angie finds a man who, she thinks, is like the ocean, which always moves.

She hopes he will give her no cause for surprise.